Out of Towners

Dan Tunstall

Five Leaves Publications

www.fiveleaves.co.uk

Out of Towners
by Dan Tunstall

Published in 2011
by Five Leaves Publications,
PO Box 8786, Nottingham NG1 9AW
www.fiveleaves.co.uk

ISBN: 978 1 907869 25 9

Five Leaves acknowledges support
from Arts Council England

Five Leaves is
represented by Turnaround
and distributed to the book trade
by Central Books

Cover photograph and design: Heron
Typesetting and design: Four Sheets Design and Print
Printed by Imprint Digital of Exeter

one

There are moments in time that you just know you're going to remember for as long as you live. This is one of them. I check my watch. It's half past two on Friday 26th of June and the National Express 677 coach is pulling into Whitbourne Bus Depot. Me, Robbie, Dylan and George are grinning like fools. It's almost too good to be true. We're sixteen. We finished our GCSEs last Friday. The summer is stretching out in front of us. And we're on our first lads' holiday. It doesn't get any better than this.

As the coach grinds to a halt, brakes hissing, Dylan stands up. He pulls his rucksack down from the rack.

"Right then boys," he says.

My stomach flips over. From the minute Robbie suggested having a weekend at his mum and dad's caravan in East Sussex when GCSEs were over, it's been about the only thing I've thought of. Which didn't help with my revision. Still, I reckon I did okay. And now the exams are done and we're actually here.

I'm the next one on my feet. It's good to be able to stretch my legs. Apart from half an hour in Victoria Coach Station in London, we've been wedged into these seats since nine o'clock this morning. All the way from Letchford. I get my bag and follow Dylan to the front of the coach. Robbie's behind me and George is at the back, stooping forward slightly so he doesn't hit his head on the ceiling.

I jump down onto the tarmac, pulling my bag onto my shoulder. The air smells of diesel fumes and oil. We stand to the side while everyone else gets off and then we wait for George to get his case out of the luggage hold. Me, Robbie and Dylan have got sports bags or rucksacks. George has got a huge bright red capsule suitcase with wheels and a handle. It's like something my uncle Keith would take on a Mediterranean cruise. As George trundles it towards us, Robbie starts to laugh.

"Can't believe you brought that."

George shrugs.

"It's practical."

I pat my pockets, checking my wallet, change, key and phone.

"Come on then," I say. "Are we getting off?"

Dylan and Robbie nod, but George is fiddling about.

"Wait a sec," he says. He stands his suitcase on its end, gets his mobile out and wanders over to where a bloke in an orange reflective jacket is brushing litter into a big yellow scuttle.

"Excuse me," George says, holding his phone out. "Could you take a photo of me and my mates?"

The bloke looks at him for a second or two. Eventually he nods.

George gives him the mobile and walks back across to us.

"Right lads. Smile for the camera."

We all stand in a line. I feel a bit of a nob.

The bloke takes the shot, hands George his phone, then gets back to his sweeping.

"Cheers," George says, but the bloke isn't listening.

George has a look at the picture. He tosses the phone to me.

"Here you go Chris. What do you think?"

I squint at the image on the screen, checking myself out. My mum reckons there's a resemblance to Jamie Redknapp. I don't know if I can see it, but I'm not unhappy with how things turned out looks-wise. My face is quite long, but my cheekbones are good, my nose is straight, my skin is clear and girls say they like my brown eyes. It's a bit vain I suppose, but I'm down here for more than the sunbathing. It's the seaside. There's going to be girls here.

I have another glance at the photo. At everyone, this time. We don't look like a gang. Me and Robbie are both about five-nine, but you've got George who's six-three, and at the other end of the scale you've got Dylan who reckons he's five-six, but he's definitely adding an inch or two. And then there's the haircuts. My brown crop, brushed up at the front, Dylan's number two, Robbie's curls, which he gets from his Jamaican mum, and George's blond Brillo pad. Even our clothes don't match. Me and Robbie are in jeans and hoodies and Etnies trainers, but Dylan's in sports gear as usual and George is in the sort of stuff only he would wear. Three-quarter-length shorts and a T-shirt with a picture of Sylvester the cat holding a surfboard. Like I said,

7

we don't look like a gang. But we are.

I chuck the phone back to George.

"It's a good shot mate," I say. "I'll get you to BlueTooth it to me later on."

George nods.

"Will do."

All the other passengers have gone now. The coach driver has closed up the luggage compartments and he's setting off for the canteen.

"Okay then," Robbie says. "Let's rock and roll."

We head for the exit. The automatic doors swish open and we're out on the streets of Whitbourne. It doesn't look much different to Letchford. Across the road there's a launderette. Mario's Washeteria. Mario's looks like it closed down a long time ago. The windows are boarded up and someone's put a brick through the Perspex sign above the door. Every dog in the surrounding area seems to have taken it in turns to crap outside the place and graffiti is daubed all over the walls. A few swastikas and *ANTHONY IS A TWAT* in big capitals.

Dylan raises his eyebrows.

"Welcome to Whitbourne," he says. "Ain't exactly St Tropez, is it?"

I laugh. Whitbourne's just a knackered little resort between Brighton and Eastbourne. It doesn't matter though. The sun's struggling to get through a bank of grey cloud. There's a bit of a wind blowing and a slight chill in the air. But there's nowhere on earth I'd rather be.

"Which way are we going then Robbie?" George asks.

Robbie rubs his nose. He doesn't answer.

8

Dylan cocks his head on one side.

"Robbie," he says. "It's your mum and dad's caravan. You know how to get there don't you?"

"Yeah yeah yeah," Robbie spits, machine-gun style. "Course I do. Just need to get my bearings. Not come here on a coach before, have I?"

A few more seconds pass. Robbie looks left and then right. A smile spreads across his face. He's got it sussed.

"Okay," he says, pointing. "It's this way. Got to tell you though, it's quite a long walk."

We set off. All the buildings on the street look the same. Two-storey, flat-roofed boxes with warped wooden cladding along the front and shops on the ground floor. Most of the shops are shut down, but a couple of spot-cash places are still open for business. We come to a corner by a big CarpetWorld. There's a sale on and someone's tied bunches of red and green balloons either side of the doorway. The car park is empty.

Turning left, we come past a red brick building. *Magistrates Court*, a sign says. A few dodgy characters are smoking on the pavement outside. At the top of the steps, a fat security guard is frisking an agitated-looking bloke in a beige Lacoste shellsuit. Seagulls are wheeling and screeching overhead, but there's still no sign of the seafront. There's still not much sign of the sun yet either. If anything, it's getting colder. I zip my hoody tight under my chin.

After a couple more minutes, Dylan starts up again.

"Shit, man," he says. "You weren't kidding about it being a long way, were you Robbie? If I'd known it was a walking holiday I'd have brought my hiking boots."

"Shut up Dylan," Robbie snaps.

He's annoying, Dylan. Always winding people up. Robbie's usually fairly laid-back, but Dylan's starting to piss him off.

As usual, George acts as the peacemaker.

"Hey you two," he says. "Stop messing."

Robbie and Dylan keep on scowling at each other, but they do what George says. George is the Voice Of Reason. He moved to Letchford from Birmingham when he was eleven. With his Brummie accent and the way he looks, he reminds me of Adrian Chiles off the telly. The one who's always banging on about West Brom.

On the face of it, George is totally different from me and Robbie and Dylan. We all play football. School teams, Sunday league, that kind of thing. We're all pretty decent players. But George is the sort who gets picked last in PE. He's such a good lad though. The soundest bloke you could ever find. And he cracks me up.

I look around, taking in a bit of the local colour. There's a cross-eyed bloke in a flat cap with a can of own-brand lager in his hand weaving our way. Outside the Health Centre over the road, a junkie is staggering up and down with a handful of prescriptions and a dog on a string. I can hear a thud-thud-thud sound coming from somewhere. Loud music on a car stereo, getting closer.

Robbie's calmed down now.

"Come on," he says. "Let's get going."

A few hundred metres further and we come to a

pedestrian crossing. We're just stepping out when we nearly get cleared up by two cars screaming past, music blasting. Before I can register what's going on, Dylan's jumped into the road grabbing his balls.

"Tossers!" he shouts.

There's a sudden screech of brakes. The cars have stopped.

Dylan lets go of his balls and gets back onto the path.

Two seconds later, six white lads are bundling out of the motors. Four from a sky blue Peugot 205, two from a black Citroen Saxo. They're a few years older than us. About eighteen to twenty. Baggy trousers, logos and chunky jewellery. They're heading our way.

"Oh shit," I say. "Great start to the weekend. A slapping from the local chavs."

We're all rooted to the spot. Running's not an option with all our luggage.

The lads from the cars are right in our faces now. A big geezer with gelled black hair and a green hoody seems to be the leader. He doesn't look the sharpest tool in the box. He's breathing through his mouth, eyes half-closed. There's a tattoo on his neck. *KIRKIE*. I assume it's his name. Having it tattooed probably comes in handy if he ever forgets what he's called.

"Got a problem?" he says, diamond earring glinting.

Dylan's straight in there. He's got a habit of acting the hard man.

"You virtually ran us over," he says.

One of Kirkie's mates pipes up. He's about Dylan's

11

height, wearing a red baseball cap. He's got the kind of acne I thought people didn't have in the twenty-first century.

"You should watch where you're going, shouldn't ya?"

Dylan's puffing out his chest, like he always does when he's in a confrontation. He's about to say something else but George steps in.

"Yeah, we're sorry," he says.

Kirkie's little mate spins round to stare at George. "You what?"

"We're sorry," George says again. "We don't want any trouble."

For some reason the lad in the cap looks like he wants to kill someone.

"Shut your mouth you lanky twat," he snarls. He seems to have taken George's height as a personal insult. It wouldn't be the first time George has ended up as a target.

Another of Kirkie's crew comes forward. He's got fag burns in his tracky bottoms and a pair of very clean fake Timberlands on. His head is the shape of one of those old-fashioned lightbulbs, hair receding at the temples. He looks at our bags and George's case. You can almost hear the cogs whirring in his brain.

"We don't like out of towners," he grunts.

I don't know why, but I find this dead funny. I bite my tongue and stare down at the ground. I look across at Robbie. He's trying not to laugh too.

"Are you two taking the piss?" the kid in the Timberlands asks.

Robbie shakes his head.

"Nah. We just want to get on our way."

There's a moment of silence. Our two gangs are sizing each other up, in case things go off.

Kirkie sniffs. He's decided it's time he took charge again.

"Anyway," he says. "We need to get this sorted, you get me? If you're staying in Whitbourne, you're going to have to pay for it."

The hairs on the back of my neck start to prickle. My hand goes to my pocket.

"You ain't having my money," I tell him. I'm not in the mood for giggling any more. I'm gearing up for a brawl.

A fat lad with buck teeth and a roll-up fag behind his ear moves towards me.

"Are you sure about that?" he says.

I take a step backwards and look at Kirkie. His expression is changing. Glancing over my shoulder, I see why. A police car has pulled up. It's a Ford Focus. A pair of coppers are getting out.

The bigger of the two policemen comes over. He's about six foot, barrel-chested and bald, with two cauliflower ears. Plays a bit of rugby in his spare time. He looks at us, and then at Kirkie and his boys.

"Are we having difficulty here, gentlemen?"

Nobody says anything.

The other copper has crossed the road now. He's shorter than his partner, with red hair combed forward. He looks closely at Kirkie.

"Callum Kirk isn't it?" he says.

Kirkie raises his chin.

The copper smiles.

13

"I hope you're keeping out of trouble, Callum. And that you're bearing in mind the advice we gave you the last time we met."

Kirkie shrugs. He looks down at his trainers. Nasty brown and cream Nikes.

The copper carries on.

"Anyway, I'm sure you and your friends have got something constructive that you could be doing. Am I right?"

Kirkie glances up.

"Yeah," he says.

Kirkie's mates are already making their way back to the cars. Kirkie follows them. He climbs into the driver's side of the Citroen Saxo. It's got fibreglass skirting round the bottom and an exhaust like an overflow pipe. On the rear bumper there's a sticker. *Driven Well? 0800 Fuck You.* Kirkie winds the window down and looks at us.

"See you around, lads," he says.

There's some revving, a thud-thud-thud as the music kicks in again, and then the cars move off. They crawl slowly up to the end of the road and round the corner. As soon as they're out of sight there's a squeal of wheels and the sound of both cars roaring away at top speed.

The two policemen give each other a world-weary look. Then the rugby-playing copper turns his attention to us.

"So you young men are here on holiday, I take it?"

"Yeah," Robbie says. "We're heading for Wonderland Holiday And Leisure World."

"First time without the parents is it?"

We all nod. I didn't think it was that obvious.

"And where have you come from?"

"Letchford," I say. "It's in Lincolnshire."

The red-haired policeman is looking at Dylan.

"How old are you all?" he asks.

A tingle goes through me. I know where this is going. If he thinks we're too young to be down here on our own, he's going to want to contact our parents. And that will mean big trouble. Because our parents don't know we're here. They're completely in the dark. We've managed to spin an intricate web of bullshit. It's pretty complicated, but basically everyone's folks thinks their lad is at someone else's house until Sunday evening. Letting off a bit of steam and chilling out after the exams. Safe and cosy back in Letchford.

"We're all eighteen," Robbie says. He sounds a bit too confident.

The coppers exchange a glance.

"I see," the red-haired one says. "You don't look eighteen. Have you got some ID on you?"

Robbie starts stuttering, trying and failing to get his words out.

I'm just getting used to the idea that the holiday's over before it's even started when I hear a crackling noise. It's the big copper's radio. He unclips it, listens for a while, then mumbles something in reply. When he's finished, he looks at us.

"Got to go lads," he says. "Duty calls."

I feel a wave of relief splashing over me. But we've not got away with it yet. The red-haired policeman is having another long hard look at Dylan.

"You chaps have a good time then," he says finally. "And take care. There's an element amongst the local fraternity who aren't so keen on visitors."

"Yeah," I say. "I think we found that out."

The coppers get back in the Focus and pull away.

I let out a big breath. Then we all start laughing.

When we've got ourselves sorted, we carry on the way we were going. We're starting to see more and more people, which I take as a sign that we're getting nearer to civilization. We take a left and we're in what looks to be the middle of Whitbourne. It's a square with block paving and benches and wooden planters full of flowers gasping for water. There's a big shopping arcade over to one side, with all the usual places. Boots. WH Smith. Costa Coffee. I can see a McDonald's down a lane to the right.

Robbie points to a signpost. Directions to the pier and seafront.

"There you go Dylan," he says. "You think your little legs can keep going for a bit longer?"

Dylan says nothing.

We cut through the town centre and the market place then head down a road filled with cafes, ice cream parlours and shops selling seaside stuff. Rock and windbreaks and buckets and spades. Up ahead, the seafront is coming into view. Everyone's gone quiet. The excitement is building. I feel like I'm five years old again. I've forgotten all about Kirkie and his mob now.

Another thirty seconds and we can see the pier. Against the backdrop of grey sea and grey sky, it's fairly rickety-looking. A jumble of wood and concrete and metal, all flaking white paint, peeling roof lead and seagull shit. It looks like one big gust of wind could send it crashing into the English Channel. But then the sun breaks through the clouds and the pier suddenly seems a whole lot more impressive.

Robbie looks at us. He points to the sky.

"How's about that for timing?"

Nobody says anything. We're too busy grinning again. The temperature seems to have gone up by five degrees in the last couple of seconds and the rays of the sun are bouncing off the surface of the sea. We all put our sunglasses on.

"Right then," Robbie says. "The lads are officially on tour. Wonderland here we come."

two

We go along the seafront, away from the pier, heading out of town. On the left of us, beyond a row of yukka plants, some fancy flowerbeds and the prom, is the beach. Grey, white, yellow and red pebbles slope gently down to the sea. Every hundred metres or so, a heavy wooden groyne stretches out into the waves. The tide is going out, but it's still quite high. It's a good time for swimming, but nobody's in the water. There's a few family groups dotted about on the stones and a bloke in big earphones ambling up and down with a metal detector, but not much else.

"Not very busy, is it?" I say.

Robbie pushes his sunglasses up his nose.

"It's not really the holiday season yet. The schools down here don't break up for weeks. It livens up at the weekends though. Londoners, mainly."

I look across to the other side of the road at the big old hotels with their fading whitewash, dirty net curtains and dusty windows staring out to sea. The Devonshire. The Heatherdene. The Glenroy. They're impressive buildings, but they've seen better days. It looks like Whitbourne was a pretty upmarket, swanky place, years ago. The glamour has faded now.

We keep going, past the bandstand, the crazy golf

and the bowling greens. After the lifeboat station there's a cluster of pine trees and then the road starts to wind uphill. Over in the distance I can see the coast curving round and climbing up towards a huge white chalk headland.

"There are some serious cliffs over there," I say.

Robbie nods.

"Yeah. The big one's called Bellevue Point. It's like Beachy Head's little brother. Hundred and twenty-five metres above sea level. It's nice up there. I've been with Mum and Dad. There's a pub and a visitors' centre. But I don't think we're going to be doing a lot of sight-seeing this weekend."

I laugh. Sight-seeing isn't too high on my list of priorities.

It's warming up now. The road away from the seafront seems to be getting steeper. I'm just thinking it's turning into another hike, when I see the gates of Wonderland looming at the end of a long road lined with tall trees.

"So what's this place like?" Dylan asks.

Robbie scratches his chin.

"Poor man's Butlins. You've got a mini-village with shops and then there's this big entertainments place where they've always got stuff going on."

I laugh.

"Knobbly-knees competitions and Glamorous Grannies?"

"You're not far off," Robbie says.

We're up at the entrance now. There's a trail of red concrete paw prints leading the way across the car park in the direction of a big grey bunker at the top of the slope. Chalets and caravans stretch away into the fields all around us.

Dylan grabs my elbow. He nods at the perimeter fence. It's five metres of mesh topped off with barbed wire.

I grin.

"Is that to keep the locals out, or keep the holidaymakers in?"

"Dunno," Dylan says.

We go through a set of double doors into the grey bunker and enter a sort of foyer area. A payphone is bolted to the wall on the right, next to a shelving unit filled with brochures for local attractions, old newspapers and dying pot plants. Straight ahead, a six-foot cardboard cut-out of a bear in red dungarees is holding a placard.

TONITE IN THE ENTERTAINMENT CENTRE
FAMILY FUN WITH COMPERE VIC WHITLEY
INTERNATIONAL DJ TONY CURTIS
SIX TIL LATE

George smiles.

"They're keen on bears," he says. "Paw prints in the car park, big cut-outs in here. What's that all about?"

"It's Benny the Bear," Robbie says. "Disneyland have got Mickey, Wonderland have got Benny."

George and Dylan nip to the toilets. I take off my sunglasses and wander across to the big notice board on the far wall. It's covered with posters for forthcoming events. There are a lot of tribute nights coming up. T-Rexocet. Stasis Quo. Seventies bands. The music my Nan listens to. Tickets are still available for Jack Jones and David Dickinson from *Bargain Hunt.*

I walk over to where Robbie's still standing and we wait for George and Dylan. When they're back, we go through another set of double doors and come out into a courtyard. It's the mini-village Robbie was talking about. There are shops to the left and right of us. The Wonderland Supermarket, a hairdressers, a chip shop, a bakers, a couple of coffee places, one or two takeaways. Across on the far side is what looks like a big sports hall. The Family Entertainment Centre.

"What do you think then?" Robbie asks.

"Spot-on mate," I say.

I have another look around. Over to the left there's a bloke leaning against the wall of the Happy Valley Chinese with a fag in his mouth. He's about sixty, and looks like he's lived every last minute. He's a dodgy-looking character in a red blazer and grey trousers that are too short for him. Under the blazer, he's wearing a purple shirt and a yellow paisley tie with a knot the size of a cricket ball. Paedo chic. He's got thin brown hair, thatched into a massive bouffant with gallons of hairspray, and a suspiciously orange tan. He sees me looking and smiles. His teeth are pearly white. Too white for a bloke of his age. A good half-inch of gum is showing under his top lip.

Dylan sees the bloke smiling at me.

"Hey, Chris. I think you've pulled."

"Piss off," I say.

We go along the row of shops on the right and then turn down a path through a field with chalets on one side and an outdoor swimming pool and adventure playground on the other. *Blue Zone*, the signs say. The skies are clearing now. The grey clouds have gone and there's just a few little fluffy white ones scudding about. The sun feels warm on my face. It's turning into a proper summer's day.

"How much further?" Dylan asks. He seems to be struggling with his rucksack. He keeps adjusting the shoulder straps.

"Not far," Robbie says.

George switches the handle of his suitcase from his left hand to his right.

"I hope this caravan's got running water," he says. "We borrowed my auntie's caravan once, and we all had to crap in a bucket."

Robbie laughs.

"Yeah. That's the sort of caravan you hitch to the back of your car. This is a static. It's luxury."

George looks chuffed.

"What's it got then?"

"Hot water on tap, electricity, gas. There's a telly, a fridge. You name it, it's in there, mate."

We're through the first field now, heading into the second. *Green Zone*. This field is full of caravans. A group of young kids is playing on a patch of grass. Two lads and two girls. They stop kicking their ball about when they see us coming. The smaller of the two lads steps out into the path. He's six or seven, with lines cut into the sides of his hair and a *Ben10* T-shirt.

"Are you here on holiday?" he asks.

"Got it in one," Dylan says.

The kid looks quite pleased with himself.

We keep on going and the kids get back to their football. Another hundred metres and we're turning right.

"Check it out," Robbie says.

I look where he's pointing. The caravan. I recognise it from his holiday photos. He's been coming here every year since he was little. *Green 64*. It looks sound. The walls are cream and white rippled metal, the windows are slightly tinted and the curtains are brown with white chevrons. Three wooden steps lead up to the door.

Robbie pulls a set of keys from his pocket. He goes up the steps, unlocks the door and heads inside. The rest of us follow him in.

It's cool in the caravan. The carpet is cream and the upholstery is oatmeal and brown tartan. The kitchen units and the storage cabinets are mock pine. The whole place smells of citrus air freshener. We go up to the far end and dump our bags, flopping onto the seats under a big window looking out across Green Zone. Robbie fumbles about under the sink in the kitchen area, making sure the gas and electricity are ready to go, and that the hot water's on. When he's finished, he comes and sits next to me.

George opens up his suitcase. He pulls out four cans of Fosters and plonks them down on the low table in front of us.

"Help yourselves," he says.

Nobody needs to be asked twice. We all crack open a can and bash them together.

"We're here lads," Robbie says.

I nod. We're here. It's properly starting to sink in now. I have a gulp of Fosters. It tastes good. I put the can back on the table.

"We almost didn't make it though," I say. "Running into those dickheads in the cars."

Robbie smiles.

"We don't like out of towners," he says, voice gruff like Kirkie's mate.

We all laugh.

Dylan shakes his head.

"They were a bunch of pussies. If the coppers hadn't turned up, we could have taken 'em."

George sighs. Me and Robbie laugh.

In his mind Dylan's one of the toughest men alive. But the fact is, he weighs about nine stone. He does a lot of exercise. Cycling, stuff like that. He's got the wiry build of one of those scrawny little riders who shoot up the mountain stages in the Tour De France. It's a good build for endurance. Not so good for fighting, I wouldn't have thought.

Dylan shrugs.

"You could see. They were all wasters. A couple of punches and that would be the end of that. Off down A&E." He stands up, rolling his shoulders, bobbing and weaving, shooting out the occasional right jab, snorting through his nose for an extra bit of impact.

I can't help cracking up.

"Do you reckon lads like that fight fair?" I ask.

"It doesn't matter if they fight fair or not. However they want to do it, they're going down." He fires out a few more jabs, leaning to one side then the other, before swinging a big right.

George tuts.

"All your ducking and diving isn't going to help you when you're drinking your dinner through a

24

straw," he says.

There's no answer to that. Dylan sits back down.

I take another swig of beer and look at my watch. Half past three. It's amazing to think that this time last week we were finishing our final GCSE. Dylan's brothers Liam and Aaron came to pick us up from Parkway College in their knackered old Ford Escort and drove us into Letchford for a celebratory pint. Me, Robbie and Dylan squashed across the back seat, George curled round in a ball in the boot. Seven days. It seems like years ago.

Robbie reaches over and puts the TV on. It's a Toshiba portable resting on top of an old silver VHS player.

Dylan's given up on the Vin Diesel act now.

"You got satellite?" he asks.

"Nah," Robbie says.

Dylan puffs out his cheeks.

"That's no good."

Robbie flicks through the channels. We end up watching *Changing Faces* on *ITV*. It's the best that's on offer. A housewife from Grimsby has been done up to look like Nicole Kidman. A style expert who's overdone the Botox is giving hints for maintaining the new image, recommending some cover-up foundation for the tattoos on the woman's hands.

It takes us about fifteen minutes to finish our beers. When we're all done, Robbie produces a roll of black bin liners from his bag. He's come prepared.

"Remember," he says, ripping a bin liner off the roll and putting the empty cans in. "There's got to be absolutely no sign we've been here."

We all nod.

A couple more minutes pass, taking it easy. I'm looking through the photos on my phone. Dylan's looking at his mobile too. He's got an iphone and it's awesome. It could probably make you a cup of tea if you asked it to. His dad owns a building firm. Cawsey Contractors. His family are rolling in cash. My mum and dad both work for the NHS. It doesn't pay quite so well. Dylan's starting work for his old man in the autumn. He's going to be loaded while the rest of us are grafting at Sixth Form.

Eventually Robbie stands up.

"Okay," he says, muting the telly. "I suppose I'd better tell you where things are in here."

I put my phone down. Dylan does the same. George has been staring out of the windows, watching the world go by, but he turns his focus back to what's happening inside the caravan.

"This is the main living and dining area." Robbie jerks his thumb over his shoulder. "Over there you've got the kitchen – gas cooker, microwave, fridge-freezer. On the left there's two bedrooms, one with a double bed, one with two singles. Then at the far end is the bathroom. In there you've got a shower, bog and sink. Like I said. Luxury."

George looks at him.

"You'd make a good caravan salesman."

"Yeah," I say. "Or an air stewardess."

Robbie looks a bit sheepish. He turns the volume back up on the TV and sits down.

Dylan scratches his earlobe.

"So who's sleeping where?" he asks.

"I thought me and Chris would go in the single beds," Robbie says. "You and George can take the double."

Dylan looks mortified.

"Why have we got to go in the double?"

"Thought you'd like it, Dylan. I know how you and George feel about each other." Robbie glances over at me. He winks.

Dylan looks like he's about to go off on one.

George reaches out and puts his hand on Dylan's knee.

"Don't worry," he says. "I'll be gentle with you."

We spend the next few minutes getting the bedrooms organised. The one I'm sharing with Robbie is a pretty tight squeeze. The whole room is only about five foot by eight. Each of the beds is two foot across, a bare mattress with a pattern of brown leaves on a wooden base. Between the beds is a gangway just wide enough to stand in. At the far end there's a little bedside cabinet and two white headboards screwed to the wall.

I throw my stuff onto the bed furthest from the door, under the window. I get my sleeping bag out, unroll it on the mattress and toss my pillow under the headboard. There's a nametag sewn into the pillowcase. *Christopher Norton.* My mum put it there when I went on a trip to Ironbridge at Primary school. I unzip the sleeping bag and turn the top down.

"Getting prepared, I see," Robbie says.

"Yeah mate. Got a feeling I might be slightly out of it by bedtime."

Robbie chucks his own sleeping bag down.

"Too right."

I stick my wash bag and towel in the bathroom,

then go into the other bedroom to see what Dylan and George are up to. Dylan's already unloaded his gear and lobbed it in a pile in the corner. I realise now why he was struggling with his rucksack. The daft twat has brought a set of weights. He's standing next to the bed doing bicep curls.

I frown.

"Shit, man. You're on your holidays."

Dylan keeps on flexing.

George is unloading his case, spreading things out over the bed. I quickly bunged a few bits in my bag before I left the house this morning. It looks like George was up all night packing. He's got four spare pairs of pants, four pairs of socks, a jumper, some T-shirts, a couple of extra pairs of trousers. He's even got some blue pyjamas. I've got one *Christopher Norton* on my pillowcase. George has got *George McKenna* plastered all over the place. Everything's neatly folded.

"My mum laid it all out for me," George says.

I pull a face.

"But she thinks you're spending the weekend at my gaff mate. Not trekking across the Andes."

George lifts an eyebrow.

"You know what my mum's like."

I leave him to it and go back out into the living area. On TV, *Changing Faces* has finished. It's a local news bulletin now. There's been a big protest about the location of a phone mast on an estate in Whitbourne. The organiser is being interviewed. In the background all the protesters are gassing into their mobiles, waving at the camera and mouthing messages.

It's nearly half past four. Everyone's back sitting around the table.

Robbie looks at us all.

"Right then," he says. "This is the million pound question. What do you want to do tonight?"

"Dunno," I say. "We could wander into town, I suppose, or we could get ourselves up to the Family Entertainment Centre. See what's going on. From the look of that poster we saw on the way in, they're having a bit of a do."

Dylan's eyes light up.

"I reckon we should stick around here. There's bound to be some talent going spare on a site this size."

I look at George.

"What do you think?"

George spreads his arms wide.

"I'm up for that if everyone else is."

Robbie's the Wonderland expert. He holds his hands out, palms upwards.

"Well," he says. "It's a bit crap in there sometimes, but we'll give it a go. What we need to do is get some supplies in to see us through to the evening. Who's going down the Supermarket?"

"I'll go," Dylan says.

Robbie's not convinced.

"I don't reckon that's a good idea. That copper in Whitbourne thought you were about twelve. If they won't sell you alcohol we're not going to have much of a night."

Dylan scowls.

I raise my hand.

"I'll go."

George yawns and stretches.

"And I'll go with him," he says.

We stand up.

"What are we getting then?" I ask.

"Cheapest booze they've got," Robbie says. "And lots of it."

three

Two other people are in the Wonderland Supermarket. One bloke, one woman. The bloke's about forty with custard-coloured hair. A bleach-job gone wrong. He's in a pair of chino shorts and a double-thickness red T-shirt with *SIGNATURE* embroidered on the front. The woman's probably early thirties. She looks like she's recently got out of bed. She's wearing a white towelling dressing gown and a pair of sky-blue fluffy slippers. They're both shuffling around aimlessly, browsing the shelves.

Me and George make straight for the back of the shop, through an aisle with bread and cakes on one side and tinned goods on the other. We know what we're after. The off-licence section. It's an impressive sight. Bitters. Lagers. Wines. Spirits. Good stuff. Cheap stuff. None of it is what we're looking for. We're looking for mega-cheap stuff. The most alcohol for the least layout. And I think I've found the answer.

"Jackpot," I say.

George looks confused.

I point to the bottom shelf.

"White Thunderbolt Cider. Three litres for two pounds sixty-nine. Five percent volume."

George is smiling.

"Now you're talking," he says.

We grab a bottle each. Job done.

"What about some food?" George asks.

He's got a point. My stomach is rumbling. None of us has eaten anything since we had some rough hot dogs from a kiosk outside Victoria Coach Station. And that was about twelve o'clock.

I shrug. Finding something to drink was easy. Finding something to eat is another thing entirely. Two minutes of wandering up and down later, and we've got four bags of Scampi Nik Naks, Four Spicy Curry King Pot Noodles and a packet of Jaffa Cakes. We look at one another and nod, satisfied. Then we head across to pay.

There are three checkouts, but only one of them is open. The woman at the till is thin with grey hair and a faded *Wrestlemania* T-shirt. She's got gold rings on every finger. Sovereigns, things that look like curtain hooks, one that says *MAM*, a green heart held between two hands.

We're third in the queue, behind the bloke in the *SIGNATURE* T-shirt. The woman in the dressing gown is up at the front. She puts a box of Pop Tarts and a pack of part-baked croissants onto the counter and asks for twenty Bensons. She's not exactly getting the week's shopping but she's paying for it with Switch and she can't get the card out of her purse. Her false nails are so long, there's no way of getting a proper grip on the edge of the plastic. By the time she's managed to get the card out and tapped her PIN number into the machine, *SIGNATURE* Man has given up. He's left his basket on the counter and set off round the shop again.

I shift my weight from one foot to the other.

"We could be here some time," I say.

I get George to BlueTooth me the picture from the Bus Depot. When that's done, I look at the tat on the shelves beside the tills. Union Jack air fresheners. A torch in the shape of a giant match with a red tip. Battery-operated hand-held fans.

SIGNATURE Man is back now. He's got himself a baguette in a long paper bag and he's trying to balance it on top of the rest of his shopping. Every time he lets go of the baguette, it slides down to one side or the other. It doesn't stop him trying.

Dressing Gown Woman has finally got her act together. She shoves her Pop Tarts into a carrier bag while the checkout operator runs the barcode reader over *SIGNATURE* Man's groceries. While he pays up, we put our bits and pieces down on the conveyor belt.

The woman at the till has clocked our six litres of cider. She looks up with suspicion in her eyes. There's an awkward couple of seconds, then she starts scanning.

"Fifteen ninety-eight," she says.

I put the shopping into two bags while George hands over a twenty and then we start the journey back.

I look at the chalets as we go through Blue Zone. They've all got white walls and peaked slate roofs. Some of them, the privately-owned ones I suppose, are like proper homes. They've got plant pots and hanging baskets and little plastic fences and a patch of lawn the size of a postage stamp. An old geezer with a terracotta tan and a load of white chest hair is pushing a mower up and down outside a chalet on the right. He's wheezing and pouring with sweat. He looks like he's going to collapse at any moment.

Further along, one or two chalets have got washing lines hung up. Giant bras and Y-fronts are swinging in the afternoon breeze. On one line there's a two-piece blue jogging suit with a trainer embroidered on the trouser leg. It's got to be the worst outfit I've ever seen.

Back at the caravan, Robbie and Dylan have hardly moved since we last saw them. They're sprawled across the seats staring at the TV. They've not even changed the channel. It's an old repeat of *Midsomer Murders*, but they seem happy enough.

I dump the bags on the table.

"Dinner is served," I say.

Dylan pushes himself upright and peers into the bag nearest to him.

"Good work," he says.

The booze and food came to virtually sixteen quid, so we all settle up with George. Four quid each. It's not made too much of a dent in the weekend's finances. I've been saving up for weeks and I've got nearly a hundred quid in my wallet.

Robbie goes across to the kitchen and fills up the kettle for the Pot Noodles, then gets four glasses out of a cupboard. He brings them across as I'm screwing the top off the first big blue bottle of cider. I pour us all some and we wait for the bubbles to die down.

"Okay then lads," I say, raising a glass. "Cheers."

The next couple of hours seem to fly by. One minute it's five o'clock, the next it's just after seven. The table's covered in empty Nik Nak packets, Pot

Noodle tubs and Jaffa Cake crumbs. We've caned one bottle of White Thunderbolt between us and we're halfway down the second. The cider is starting to take effect. As I stand to go to the toilet for the second time in the last half hour, the caravan seems to take a little lurch to one side.

When I get back from the bog, *Emmerdale* is on. I'm really beginning to appreciate the fact we've got *Sky* at home.

"Isn't there anything better than this?" I ask.

Robbie picks up the remote. He flicks through all five channels.

"Not looking good."

George waves his cider glass at the VHS machine.

"Got any videos?"

"Nah," Robbie says.

Dylan butts in.

"Tell you what we need. Some porn." He burps. "If I'd have known there was a video player I could have nicked one of Liam's tapes. I know where he keeps them."

I bite my tongue. Dylan's record in providing porn isn't good. He once brought a tape round to my house that he'd got at a car boot sale. He'd paid a fiver for it. XXX-rated stuff, or so he thought. It turned out to be *Antiques Roadshow*. We fast-forwarded all the way to the end, but it was pointless. No naked women. We did see some great furniture and porcelain though.

Robbie puts *Emmerdale* back on. A few minutes pass. I look out of the window. More and more people are heading towards the Family Entertainment Centre. It started around six with dribs and drabs. Now there's a steady flow. I pour myself another drink.

"Suppose we'd better start getting ourselves sorted," I say.

There's some grunting and nodding of heads.

Dylan gets up.

"I'll go first. Then George can be next. We're proper men. We won't take ages in the bathroom. Not like you pair of girls." He points at me and Robbie. "I know how long you two need fiddling with your hair."

He's right. But styling hair isn't an issue with Dylan and George. Dylan's hair is never more than half an inch long, and George has got hair that you can't do anything with. It sits there on his head like a dodgy wig.

"We're metrosexuals, mate," I say.

"You're what?"

I decide not to bother explaining.

Dylan doesn't take long in the bathroom. Five minutes and he's back out again, top off, Letchford Town towel thrown over his shoulder.

"Who's is this?" he asks, holding up a bottle of aftershave.

"It's mine," Robbie says. "Careful. It cost forty quid."

I laugh.

"It didn't you know. His mum won it down the bingo."

Dylan smirks and heads off to get his going-out clobber on.

George finishes another glass of cider then pushes himself up out of his seat. As he puts one foot in front of the other, he staggers slightly and almost overturns Robbie's mum's big vase of dried bulrushes.

"Whoa," he says. "Who's done that to my legs?"

I shake my head. George is pissed.

He straightens up the vase then goes off to take his place at the sink.

Another five minutes and it's my turn. As I'm washing I check myself out in the mirror. Still looking good. Me and Robbie are definitely the heartthrobs around here, as my Nan would say. The only difference is, he's gone all the way with a couple of girls and I haven't. I've had two quite steady relationships. Abbie. Eleanor. Things have never developed though. Don't know why. Just hasn't happened. And now I'm young, free and single. We all are.

I dry my face, put some anti-spot cream across my nose and chin, then rub in a bit of moisturiser. I brush my teeth and spray on some deodorant. I get my own bottle of aftershave and dab a bit on. Issey Miyake. I nicked it off my dad.

I brush my hair through once or twice, then I go into my full routine. Five minutes of poking and tweaking and it's looking spot-on. Waxed and smooth on the back and sides, spiked on top. At home, my sister Beth takes the piss out of the amount of time I spend on my appearance. She reckons it's a sign of Obsessive-Compulsive Disorder. But that's what A-Level Psychology does to you. In our house you can't do anything without Beth psychoanalysing you. And she's missing the point anyway. To look this good takes effort. I have a last

37

peek in the mirror, blow myself a kiss and push the door open.

"Bathroom's all yours," I tell Robbie.

In the bedroom I strip down to my boxers and socks and get a mauve polo shirt and another pair of jeans out of my bag. I'm not sure what the dress code is for Friday nights at Wonderland. Judging by the people I saw heading down to the Family Entertainment Centre, it's Hawaiian shirts and sandals. I'm not up for that, but I reckon this outfit should be okay.

I stick my Etnies back on, get my phone, my change and my wallet and duck into Dylan and George's bedroom to see how I'm looking in the full-length mirror on the wardrobe doors. Not bad. Not bad at all. As a final touch I go back to my bag and get a couple of bangles from the end pocket. One brown leather, one black and white beads.

Out in the living area, Dylan and George are watching telly. They've flicked over to *Five* and they're watching a fly-on-the-wall documentary about swearing kids and scummy parents. George is in a white open-necked shirt tucked into black trousers. Typical George. He's about to go out on the lash and he's dressed like an insurance salesman. Dylan's in a pair of baggy combats and his Letchford Town shirt. Bright orange with Leroy Lewton's number 16 on the back. He's not going to be winning any fashion awards either. I sit down, pour myself another glass of cider and we all wait for Robbie.

It's nearly eight-fifteen by the time he emerges. Five more minutes in the bedroom and he's finally ready. He's in a tight white T-shirt and jeans. He looks good, and he knows it.

He's got male-model looks, Robbie. His mum's black and his dad's white, and he seems to have got the best bits of both of them. His skin's a kind of coffee-colour and his hair is cool. It's long and curly, halfway between an Afro and dreads. He's pretty fashion-conscious and he's always wearing good gear. Last year, in the girls' bogs at school, someone wrote *Robbie Swann Is Well Fit*. Robbie was chuffed about that. He went on about it for months. I reckon he sneaked in there and wrote it himself. He takes a seat and fills up his tumbler. The cider has almost gone now.

"We going to get some action tonight then?" Dylan asks.

"With a bit of luck," I say.

Robbie swings his foot against mine.

"Yeah Chris. It's about time you broke your duck."

Dylan bursts out laughing, choking on his cider.

"I can't get over you still not popping your cherry," he says, between splutters.

I twist my face into a half-smile. I don't give a monkey's, but I don't see why he's having a go at me. It's not as if I'm the only one who hasn't scored yet. George hasn't. And, come to think of it, neither has Dylan as far as I know.

Dylan's still gurgling away like a blocked drain.

"Give it a rest Dylan mate," I say. "You're as much of a virgin as I am."

The laughing stops. Dylan's mega-serious.

"Shut it Chris."

I put down my glass. George and Robbie are looking at us both.

"So what are you saying then Dylan? You've done the business have you?"

Dylan's chest is swelling up. He's more aggressive than usual now he's got some alcohol inside him.

"Yeah," he says. "You know I have. The bird I met on holiday last summer. She lives up in Manchester, but I've seen her a couple of times since."

I give George and Robbie a wink. Dylan's Legendary 'Bird From Manchester'.

Dylan keeps going. He's sounding defensive now.

"Don't pretend you don't know what I mean. I told you about it."

"How come this bird never comes to Letchford then?" Robbie asks. "How come we never see her?"

"Yeah," I say. "We don't know what she looks like. We don't even know her name."

A grin is spreading across Robbie's face.

"I do," he says. "It's Pam. Pam of his hand."

Dylan bangs his cider down on the table.

"Tossers," he says.

George doesn't like the way things are heading.

"Let's stop messing," he says.

It all goes quiet. George to the rescue again. He's like a single parent with three out-of-control kids. Me and Robbie are the slightly more mature older brothers and Dylan's the little jug-eared one running wild on E numbers and Ritalin.

On the telly, some social-worker-type in ginger brogues is diagnosing the scruffy family's problems. They need to work on their communication skills. Behind where he's standing, the husband and wife are screaming abuse at each other while their pet Staffy goes round in a figure of eight trying to chew

40

its tail off.

I open and close my phone. No texts. No missed calls. Good. I was worried my mum might be trying to check up on me. I pick up the cider bottle one more time and splash the last drops evenly between the four tumblers on the table. We all drink up and get to our feet. It's half past eight. Time to go.

four

The sun is just beginning to go down as Robbie locks up and we start on our way to the Family Entertainment Centre. The sky over to the right, out across the sea, is turning pink. We wander to the end of our row and turn left along the path through Green Zone.

As we walk I catch sight of us reflected in caravan windows. For the second time today, I think what a funny-looking gang we are. Different heights, different clothes. At Parkway College, lots of kids are into dressing like they're in a tribe. Townies. Chavs. Moshers. Football Lads. We're not like that. Me and Robbie look a bit Skater Boy, but not too much. Maybe our trademark is that we haven't got a trademark.

The four kids we saw earlier are still out and about. They see us and run across, walking alongside.

The oldest girl, who looks about eight, wrinkles her nose.

"You boys smell of perfume," she says.

I laugh.

"It's not perfume. It's aftershave."

The girl nods. She's in Harry Potter pyjamas and a pair of pink cowboy boots.

The youngest lad picks his nose, rolls the bogey

between his fingers and drops it on the grass.

"Are you going to try to pull tonight?" he asks.

"Absolutely," Dylan says.

We keep walking. The kids have stopped following now.

"Bet you don't pull," one of them shouts.

"Cheeky bastards," Robbie mumbles.

Behind us there's the sound of sniggering.

We leave Green Zone and cut through the Blue Zone field. Two little lads are still in the adventure playground, swinging on the monkey bars, but the swimming pool is deserted. Quite a few people are outside the Family Entertainment Centre. There's fifteen or twenty smokers huddled over to the left, three youths tooling about on bikes, and a man and woman in unofficial-looking England clobber working their way through a pile of scratch cards.

The doors of the Entertainment Centre are open so we go straight in. My eyes take a while to adjust to the gloom. When they do, I start to pick out a few details. It's a huge place, extending down to the left and ending with a raised stage that's closed off by a pair of maroon curtains. In the far corner is a DJ booth, empty at the moment. There's a bar all along the right-hand wall and hatches serving food dotted along the wall facing us. The middle of the room is filled with holidaymakers grouped around tables. Up near the front is a space for dancing. There's a low murmur of talking, mixed in with the odd shout, and the chink of glasses and cutlery.

We head down towards the stage, looking for somewhere to sit. Soon we've got ourselves a table and four chairs. I look around to see who we're sitting near. I'm hoping there might be some girls about. It's not too promising. On one side of us is a big lumpy family in head-to-toe towelling gear. The mother's got a bandaged leg propped up on a chair and the kids are trying to make a shagged-out Alsatian drink beer from their dad's pint glass. On the other side, a fat woman in yellow-rimmed glasses is holding the hand of a terrified-looking lad with a backwards cap and wispy facial hair. He looks younger than us. It's the world's crappest toyboy.

"Right then," Robbie says. "Who's getting the beers in?"

Everyone looks at George.

"Go on then," he says. "I'll get them, but I'll need someone to give me a hand."

Robbie and Dylan seem strangely fascinated by their mobiles, so I stand up.

"I'm there," I say.

It's busy as we try to get served. The floor of the hall is polished wood, but there's carpet near the bar area. It's so sticky, every time my foot comes off the ground it makes a noise like someone unfastening a piece of Velcro. Or it would do if I could hear anything above the sound of *Agadoo*. International DJ Tony Curtis has started his set. I don't think it's going to be cutting-edge stuff.

George is the tallest bloke in the room and he stands out a mile, so it's not long before we've got someone's attention. I'm a bit nervous about us being asked our age, but not a lot. The White Thunderbolt has taken the edge right off my anxiety.

"Four pints of Carling," George says.

The barmaid is a middle-aged woman in a sleeveless white top. She's got a Taz tattoo on her upper arm and blonde permed hair tied in a bunch on top of her head. She doesn't even bother to look up. She just pours the drinks, takes George's money and hands him his change.

George looks at me and winks. He hands me two pints and gets the other two himself.

We weave back to our table and sit down.

Robbie picks up his pint.

"Any problems?"

"Piece of cake," George says. "Two pound sixty-five a pint, mind you."

I look across at Tony Curtis's DJ booth. It's like a picnic table with an awning over the top, spray-painted black. There are two signs like car numberplates screwed to the front.

INTERNATIONAL DJ
TONY CURTIS

Two sets of multicoloured disco lights are twirling on either side. Tony is a fat bloke with spiky hair, wearing a white *Mens' Health* T-shirt. One of those ones they give away free when you take out a subscription. His beer gut is hanging out underneath, and every now and then he tries to shrug the T-shirt down so less flesh is on show. *Agadoo* is finished, and Tony is giving a big shout out to the Kettering Posse.

Dylan pulls a face.

"What makes him an International DJ?"

"He once went on a day trip to Calais," I say.

Tony Curtis's DJ set goes on for the next twenty minutes. It's a shocker. *The Birdie Song. Oops Upside Your Head. The Lion Sleeps Tonight.* Eighties hell. When he wants to get right up to the minute, he puts on *Livin la Vida Loca.* It's not only the Kettering Posse he's giving a big shout out to. It's the Leicester Boys and the Colchester Crew.

I nudge Robbie.

"Go and get him to play something for the Letchford Lads. See if he's got any Westlife."

Robbie grins.

It's getting hot in the Family Entertainment Centre. The whole room is packed out now. The only fresh air is getting in through some little windows high up along the side walls, and a couple of sky-lights. Me and George have another trip to the bar to get the drinks in. Dylan's paying this time. As I sink into my chair, I can feel sweat trickling down my sides. I slide my phone open. Coming up to half past nine.

Tony Curtis fades out the last few bars of *Is This the Way to Amarillo?* His disco lights have stopped twirling. The three people on the dance floor shuffle back to their tables.

We all look at one another. Something's about to happen.

"Okay, you wacky Wonderlanders," Tony says, voice rising to build up the excitement. "We're going to have a change of pace now. I'm sure you're going to love this. It's our host with the most, TV favourite, our very own VIC WHITLEY!"

The room is plunged into complete darkness, then

the maroon curtains roll back and Vic Whitley bounds onto the stage. I recognise him straight away. It's not because I've seen him on TV. It's his clothes that are familiar. The red blazer and the grey trousers. It's the bloke we saw outside Happy Valley, smoking. The one who looked like a sex offender.

"How are you doing?" he bellows. He's picked up a microphone on a stand from somewhere but he hasn't managed to switch it on. He fiddles for a while, then tries again. "Whitbourne Wonderland - how are you doing?"

There's a sort of grunt from the crowd, but it's good enough for Vic.

"Before we go any further," he says, "I've got someone I want you all to meet. He's my cheeky partner in crime, the kiddies' favourite. Ladies and gentlemen, boys and girls, here he is, the Wonderland Holiday And Leisure World mascot, Benny the Bear."

The music for *Teddy Bears' Picnic* comes on, a door opens over by the bar and a man in a furry suit and dungarees starts to make his way through the audience, dancing around, patting people on the head. Benny gets to the front and hauls himself onto the left-hand edge of the stage as the music fades out.

With Benny's grand entrance taken care of, Vic launches into his spiel.

"What do you get if you cross a mouse with an elephant?" he barks.

There's no response. I can hear a few groans. Vic's stepping from foot to foot, desperate to deliver the punchline. He's got a burn mark on the shoulder of his blazer, like someone's stubbed a fag out on him.

"Big holes in your skirting boards," he says.

There's a faint sound of laughter from the far right corner, but as I look across, I see that it's because a bloke in an Arsenal shirt has spilt his pint all over his trousers.

George rolls his eyes.

"When was this bloke on the TV?"

"*Sunday Night at the London Palladium*, 1973," Robbie says.

George laughs.

Robbie's expression doesn't change.

"I'm not joking."

Fifteen minutes into Vic's act and things are pretty grim. Because it's a family show, Vic's material is on the limited side. There's the odd mother-in-law joke, but cabaret-type stuff and sexual references are definitely not on the agenda. The latest gag involves Mickey Mouse, Minnie Mouse and a rabbit-shaped jelly mould. A couple of the kids near the front are crying. Sections of the crowd look like they're losing the will to live.

Some people are having fun though. The over-sixty-fives are lapping it up. It took them a while, but now they're all well away. One woman over to the far left is in hysterics. She's honking and bellowing like a sealion, slapping her hand against her knee.

Dylan looks at me.

"Tell you what," he says. "If she keeps on like that, she's going to burst her colostomy bag."

Vic's routine drags on and on. While he's going

through his repertoire, Benny the Bear is cavorting at the side of the stage, interacting with the under-fives. He's having a bad time. At one point, a little lad creeps up behind him and squats down while his mate goes in front of Benny and pushes him backwards. Benny goes down hard and his head nearly comes off, but he springs back up and carries on bouncing around.

Ten more minutes and the show is finally finished. There's a bit of half-hearted clapping from the bulk of the crowd, and a standing ovation from the bus-pass-holders. Vic and Benny take a bow. The bloke who spilt his pint has stripped down to his pants now, and he's dancing in front of a couple of women in matching *Over Forty and Still Naughty* T-shirts. He's grabbing his crutch and swinging his hips backwards and forwards. It seems to be going down well.

Vic starts gesturing for the clapping to stop. It already has.

"Thank you, thank you," he's saying. "You're too kind, you really are."

Benny the Bear shambles off backstage. Vic bows to the audience one last time and exits stage left. There's a whine of feedback, then *Agadoo* comes on again. A couple of old dears get up and start dancing.

I look around. Another check to see if any girls have arrived. Still no joy. The fat woman in the glasses and her toyboy are snogging now, grappling with each other. I shake my head and stand up.

"I'm off for a piss," I say.

The toilets are full. A crowd of blokes three-deep

is waiting for the urinals, so I head for the nearest of the four locked cubicles. After a few seconds there's a sound of flushing and the door swings open. It's Benny the Bear. He's got a can of Tennent's Super in one paw, and he's got his bear head under his arm. Benny's a red-faced fat man with a skinhead. He takes a swig of his can and looks at me.

"I fucking hate kids," he says.

When I've taken a long piss, I make my way back through the hall. I'm scouting for girls, but I'm still drawing a blank. Most of the women in the place are about fifty. A lot of them look like they should be working as a landlady in one of the soaps. Tony Curtis has returned to his booth. He's opened his latest stint with *Come On Eileen*, more eighties rubbish, and he's put a smoke machine on. There's so much smoke billowing, I'm half-expecting the sprinklers to get triggered off. Although come to think of it, this place probably doesn't have sprinklers.

As I sit down I notice I'm getting close to the bottom of my second pint. When you add in the can and the cider, I've had quite a lot to drink I suppose. The walk down here sobered me up a bit, but I'm feeling light-headed now. My face is hot and I can feel my pulse in my temples.

Dylan's looking really pissed off.

"Cheer up mate," I say.

Dylan gestures with his glass.

"Look at this place," he says. "It's ten o'clock and we've not even had a sniff of a nice bird. It's Grab-a-Granny night."

I have a mouthful of Carling.

"You wanted to come here. You thought there would be some talent."

Dylan snorts.

"Bollocks," he says. "Don't try to pin it on me."

I switch my attention to Robbie. He doesn't look much happier than Dylan. He's shifting about in his chair, craning his neck to look over the heads of the people around us.

"What's up with you?" I ask.

"I'm getting paranoid about seeing someone who knows my mum and dad," Robbie says.

I can't say anything to reassure him, so I say nothing. The evening is going downhill fast. Looking up, I see George wandering across towards us. He's got a tray with four pint glasses on it. There's something strange about these pints. They're completely see-through.

George plonks the tray on the table and sits down.

There's a sinking feeling in my guts.

"George," I say. "That's not what I think it is in those glasses is it?"

George has got his serious face on.

"It's water, Chris. We need to be sensible. We've been boozing for hours. We've got to stay hydrated."

I shake my head in disbelief. Robbie and Dylan are doing the same. The thing is though, nobody can be bothered to argue. We down the pints in silence. The night has reached a new low. All sorts of thoughts are floating in circles in my brain. I need to think of something to lift the mood. We can't be sitting here sipping water, feeling sorry for ourselves. This is our first ever real lads' night out.

There's some movement on the far side of the

family with the Alsatian. A hen party has turned up. Six women in their thirties done up in French maid outfits and flashing red devil horns. They all look like they've had a few. The bride-to-be has got an L-plate taped to the front of her apron and a bottle of WKD in her hand. She takes a big swig and passes out on the table top.

I have a second quick peek. I'm trying to be subtle, but I get caught. A short woman with one of those haircuts that's smooth at the front and spiked up at the back has seen me. She starts waving. I raise a hand, then pick at the edge of the table.

Robbie looks more animated.

"Who are you waving at?" he asks.

"Table full of women over there," I say.

Robbie twists round in his seat.

"Shit," he says. "Cougars."

I don't get it.

"You what?"

"Cougars," Robbie says. "It's what they call middle-aged women out on the pull for younger lads. I read it in the Sunday papers."

I nod slowly.

"Right."

I have another look across and immediately get spotted again. Another wave. I stare at the floor, glad that it's dark so that no-one can see me blushing. I'm starting to feel uncomfortable sitting here. *Come On Eileen* finishes and the next track booms out. *I Predict A Riot*. It's the first half-decent song I've heard all evening

I jump up. It's a flash of inspiration. A way out of being stuck here like a rabbit in the headlights.

"Come on," I shout. "Stop moping. Dancing time."

Before anyone can argue, I've barged my way onto the dance floor. Luckily, when I turn round, the rest of the lads have followed me.

I wouldn't call what goes on for the next four minutes dancing. It's more like jumping around, bumping into people. It's still brilliant though. By the time the song ends, we're all pissing ourselves laughing. The night is finally on course. Tony Curtis is cueing up the next song and I'm hoping it's another good one.

"Righty-ho then Whitbourne," Tony says. "I call this part of the night The Erection Section. I think all you boys and girls know what I'm talking about. It's time for some slowies. This is a little number I know you're going to remember. It's those Take Thatters, and they're looking to *Rule The World*."

Dylan looks completely disgusted. He's back at our table in under five seconds. The rest of us are following, but a group of women is blocking our way. The hen party. Before I know what's happening, I've been grabbed by the wrists and dragged over in the direction of the DJ booth by the woman who's been waving at me. When we're in a bit of space she throws her arm round my neck and puts her other hand on my waist. Her wedding ring glints in Tony Curtis's flashing lights.

"Hiya love," she shouts over the music. "I'm Bev."

five

I'm sure *Rule The World* only lasts about four minutes, but it's turning into the longest four minutes of my life. As Take That warble on and on, Bev's embrace starts getting tighter. She's got me by the hips and she's pulling me closer, moving up and down. I look around in panic. To the left George is being manhandled by a big woman with frizzy black hair. Robbie's dance partner is about as tall as him, skinny, wearing an ankle chain. I see Robbie looking and I mouth the word *help*. Robbie laughs and shakes his head.

I look at Bev, trying to work out my next move. She smiles at me, but her eyes aren't focussing properly. She leans into my shoulder. I can feel her breath on my cheek.

"I didn't get your name, love," she says.

I gulp.

"Er, I'm Chris," I say, trying to sound confident.

Bev nods.

"Yeah love. I'm pissed too."

The song is winding down. I try to wriggle free, but Bev's having none of it. *Eternal Flame* is coming on, and her hands are moving round to my arse. For the next couple of minutes we teeter about on the dance floor, locked together by Bev's vice-like grip. It's like running a three-legged race on drugs.

Bev gives me another unfocussed smile. She leans in again.

"You're a good-looking boy," she whispers. "How about coming back to the chalet with me?"

I open and shut my mouth, but no words come out. In a way I'm flattered. But I'm terrified too. Bev would eat me alive. I snatch another glance at Robbie, just as he looks my way. The bastard is laughing so hard he's almost bent double.

"Nah. I'd better stay with my mates," I croak.

Bev isn't put off.

"Don't be shy," she says.

Bev has let go of my arse now and she's fumbling around with my hands. I look down to see what she's up to. She's got a pair of plastic handcuffs covered in pink furry stuff. One end is attached to her wrist. She's trying to attach the other end to me.

I step back and pull my hands out of the way. The song is almost finished, so I make a break for it. George and Robbie have had the same idea. We all leg it towards our table, expecting to see Dylan. But Dylan isn't there. I look back across at the dance floor. Bev doesn't seem to be too bothered I've done a runner. She's already latched onto one of the Leicester Boys Tony Curtis was giving a shout out to earlier. A big fat chap in a white cap-sleeve T-shirt with grey panels under the armpits to show off the sweatstains. They're grinding away to *Unchained Melody*.

George blows out a huge breath.

"Bloody hell," he says.

I know how he feels.

"I've never been so scared," I say.

Robbie strokes his chin.

"I don't know what's up with you two. I was getting into that."

We all crack up.

When we've been sitting down for a couple of minutes, I start looking around for Dylan. I'm assuming he must have gone to the toilet. But if that's where he's been, he's had a busy time. Because he's heading over here now, and he's not on his own. He's with a gorgeous Asian girl. She looks like one of the classy Townies at school. She's in a little black dress and ballet pumps. She's got silky shoulder-length hair, a flawless complexion and a gold stud in her nose. She's so pretty, she doesn't look real.

Dylan's grinning like he's won the Lottery. He pulls a spare chair across to our table and motions for the Asian girl to sit down.

"Boys," he says. "This is Nikita. Nikita, this is Chris, Robbie and George."

Nikita smiles and we all nod our heads like the dog in the Churchill Insurance adverts, lost for words.

Robbie's the first to snap out of it.

"Alright Nikita?" he says. "You here on your own?"

"No," Nikita says. She's got a slight London accent. "I'm here with my friends Steph and Gemma. They're just coming."

I look over in the direction Nikita's facing. Two girls are cutting across from the bar, bottles in hands. One is tall with sandy-coloured, slightly wavy hair. She's in a purple blouse and a pair of skinny jeans. She's not bad looking, but she's a bit straight. Not my type. I can't see the other girl yet.

She's a pace or two behind the tall one. But as they move closer, I get my first proper look at her. My jaw drops open. She's incredible.

My brain is processing information super-fast. About five-three. Rolling Stones T-shirt and black jeans. Nice skin. Wide mouth. Perfect teeth. Shiny brown hair, loosely tied up. Beautiful without even trying. Something in her body language says she's the boss of her gang. Don't know what it is. It's the way she carries herself. Inner confidence.

I swing into action, grabbing two extra seats and sliding them across. The girls are here now, and they both nod at me as they see what I'm doing. I catch the smaller girl's eye and my heart leaps.

I sit back down, trying not to stare. I hope my tongue's not hanging out. In the space of the last sixty seconds, the night has turned into something completely different.

Dylan looks round at us all. His grin is showing no signs of fading. He takes a breath and launches into another set of introductions, pointing each of us out in turn, shouting to be heard over the sound of Mariah Carey on the PA.

"Okay girls," he says. "This is Robbie. This is George. And this is Chris. Robbie, George and Chris, meet Gemma and Steph."

Steph. Her name's Steph. Like a plank, I reach my hand out to shake. Steph takes it, giggling. A jolt of electricity goes through me.

"Chris Norton," I stutter. My mouth is dry. I let go of Steph's hand and have a swig of beer.

"Steph Warner," Steph says. She's got a soft voice and an accent like Nikita. "Dylan says you're all

57

from Letchford?"

"Yeah," I say. "Where are you from?" It's the best I can manage. I wish I'd had a bit more to drink.

"We're down here from Streatham. We've just finished our GCSEs. We're staying at Gemma's granddad's chalet. Got here this morning. No-one knows, back home. My mum would kill me if she knew where I was."

I can hardly get my head round what I'm hearing.

"No way," I say. "Same as us. We're in Robbie's parents' caravan. We're dead if anyone finds out."

Steph smiles, shaking her head. Up close she's even better-looking. A bit like Cheryl Cole, or Tweedy, or whatever she calls herself nowadays. Something about her nose and her eyes. Or perhaps it's not her eyes, it's the shape of her eyebrows. I don't know. Whatever. She's mega-fit.

The night is sailing along now. Me and Steph are talking about loads of different things. I manage to slip into conversation the fact that I'm not seeing anyone at the moment. Steph isn't either. We've got stuff in common. Bands and books and TV shows we both like.

Fifteen minutes pass in what feels like five seconds. Right from the word go, everyone's getting on. It's funny. We don't look like a gang, and neither do they. They're different shapes and sizes, they're dressed differently, but somehow they work together.

Me and Robbie go to the bar to get another round in. Pints for us, Smirnoff Ice for the girls. Robbie's a lot happier now. He's not worrying about bumping into someone who knows his parents any more.

As we sit down again, I look at George. You can see he's into Gemma in a big way. George is usually hopeless around girls. Whenever they talk to him at school, he gets nervous, starts biting his bottom lip. Then he gets all clumsy and uncoordinated. Sure enough, he's biting his lip now, but he's not fallen over or spilt his drink yet. He looks like he's doing alright. Whatever he's saying, Gemma keeps nodding and smiling.

Across on the other side of the table, Dylan and Nikita are laughing about something.

I lean towards Steph.

"Nikita's enjoying herself," I say.

Steph drinks from her bottle.

"Yeah. She's letting her hair down this weekend. Her mum and dad are pretty strict. What they don't know isn't going to hurt them though."

I'm busting for the toilet. I leave Steph in charge of my pint while I head off.

It's not as packed in the toilets as it was earlier, so I go straight across to the urinals. When I'm finished, I turn round and see someone familiar coming in. Tangerine football shirt. Dylan. He heads for the condom machine and stands there looking thoughtful. He's not spotted me. I creep up and poke him in the ribs.

"Dylan, you sad bastard. You met her less than half an hour ago."

Dylan spins round, shoving coins into his pocket. Different emotions pass across his face, one after the other. Surprise. Confusion. Guilt. Within two seconds, he's back to his usual self. He gives me a wolfish look.

"You've got to be prepared," he says. "This is why you never get laid."

I grunt.

"So you think she's going to get 'em off then, do you?"

Dylan's full of himself.

"Never underestimate The Cawsey Boy. Tonight is Nikita Kaur's lucky night."

"Get real Dylan," I say. "A bird like that isn't going to drop and go for it. She's got more self-respect."

Dylan shrugs.

"Maybe. But she came and spoke to me. Not the other way round."

"Meaning?"

"Meaning she must have liked what she saw. And who can blame her?"

I grunt again and leave him to it. There's no arguing with Dylan's logic.

Out in the hall, I slalom through the holidaymakers back to our table. I've thought of something funny I can tell Steph. But there's a problem. Robbie's shifted into my seat and he's turning on the charm. A sick feeling starts to churn inside me.

It's not surprising that Robbie's making his move. George and Gemma already look like they're paired up, and so do Dylan and Nikita. Which leaves me and Robbie competing for Steph. I suppose I knew it already. I just hoped it wouldn't come to that. The thing is, me and Robbie have got a bit of history when it comes to fancying the same girls. Becky. Natalie. There's one or two others. And Robbie always seems to come out on top. Robbie's my best mate. But sometimes he's my biggest enemy.

I sit back down and try to act casual. George and Gemma are still locked in conversation, so I lean across and chat to Nikita until Dylan comes back from the toilets. I wonder what he's got hidden in his pockets. I flash him a sideways glance, but he's giving nothing away. He gets talking with Nikita again. I look over at Robbie and Steph, seeing if there's any way I can butt in. It's not looking good. Robbie's doing all he can to avoid my gaze. I'm starting to feel left out when Tony Curtis throws me a lifeline.

At last, the Erection Section is coming to an end. I reckon it's been at least three quarters of an hour. For most of the time it's been a pre-recorded CD playing automatically while Tony's crammed his face with chips, standing outside the Fire Exit with a fag in his hand. But now he's back, and he's opening his new set with some Killers. *Somebody Told Me*. It's not exactly a recent release, but at least it was recorded in our lifetimes, unlike the other dross he's been playing.

Steph's face lights up. She gets to her feet, grabs my hands and drags me out of my chair.

"Come on," she says.

My night is instantly in gear again. I'm well chuffed. We're on the dance floor in seconds flat. Robbie's following, but you can see he's pissed off. This doesn't usually happen to him.

Soon all seven of us are up giving it loads, and we keep it going for most of the next forty minutes, with the odd pitstop for toilet breaks. Tony Curtis's music is much better now. It's pretty much all from the twenty-first century. There's no awkwardness when we're dancing. It's not like anyone's together in a couple. We're all just having a good laugh. And it gives me a chance to properly check Steph out.

It's closing in on midnight. All the kids have gone to bed. Most of the people in the Family Entertainment Centre are utterly wrecked. A fair few of them have probably been here since six o'clock. The atmosphere is getting rowdy and it's not long before a massive fight starts off to the side of the dance floor.

It's hard to see what's going on with the flashing lights and Tony Curtis's smoke machine working flat-out. Basically though, it's members of the Kettering Posse and the Colchester Crew having a turf war. Someone's sat in the wrong seat and it's all gone ballistic. A table has been turned over and bottles have started flying about.

Tony Curtis is oblivious to it all. He's put on *Y.M.C.A.*, and he's doing the dance, in a little world of his own. Everyone else knows what's going on though. People have started running for cover. Women are screaming and there's a big space opening up in the middle of the hall with various tubby blokes thundering about, trying to hit each other and falling over. It's quite funny.

But then I look across at Steph. Steph's not laughing. There's a strange expression on her face I haven't seen before. Partly frightened, partly sad. I click into protective mode, putting my arm round her waist and steering her away to the far side of the room.

Tony's finally caught on to what's happening. He

turns the music off and starts appealing for calm, without much success. The fighting shows no signs of stopping. A pint glass sails over and shatters against the side of the DJ booth.

We're all standing in the corner now.

Steph shakes her head.

"I hate violence," she says. "It spoils everything."

Another glass arcs through the air.

"Let's get out of here," I say. "I've had a brain-wave."

"What's that then?" Robbie asks.

"We should go down to the beach."

Dylan looks at me like I've gone mad.

"It'll be a laugh," I say.

One by one, everyone starts to nod their head. It's a daft idea, a spur-of-the-moment thing, but it looks like we're all up for it.

Robbie clears his throat.

"Right then," he says. "Let's rock and roll."

Skirting round the side of the people still scuffling, we go out of the main doors and into the courtyard. It's nice to be in the fresh air. It was like a sauna in the Family Entertainment Centre. The Supermarket and most of the other shops are closed up for the night, but all the takeaways are open and doing good business. Outside Happy Valley a group of women are gathered around, taking it in turns to pat and rub the back of their mate who's emptying her stomach onto the pavement.

Gemma's got something on her mind.

"Just a mo," she says.

There's not time to ask what she's up to. She's off into Blue Zone with Nikita.

I look at Steph and raise my eyebrows. Steph shrugs.

It's not long before Gemma and Nikita are back. Gemma's holding a canvas bag. I can hear a clinking sound, like glass. A quick peek in the top of the bag confirms it. Two half-full bottles of vodka.

"Gemma, you're a star," I say.

Gemma curtseys.

We're ready to go. We nip straight through the foyer, blinking against the glare of the strip lights. On the other side, we go across the car park and through the gates. There's no traffic about, so we walk in the middle of the road like a group of gun-fighters on the way to a showdown.

Whitbourne is gradually coming into view down below us. Rows of orange streetlights cut across one another and white lights glow from the buildings. Over to the right, lit up like a Christmas decoration, the pier juts out into the sea. The sea itself is inky black and glistening, reflecting a moon that's probably a day off being full. The sky is clear, with a few splodges of cloud. There are more stars out tonight than I've ever seen.

The walk down into town is a lot easier than the uphill slog we had this afternoon. Nobody's saying much. It feels like we're off on a big adventure, and if we say anything we might spoil it. Before long we're coming to the end of the seafront road, with the hotels to one side and the beach on the other. Somewhere in the town I can hear a clock striking half past midnight. We go past the bandstand, then down a flight of concrete steps to the prom. Fifty metres further, another flight of steps, and we're on the beach.

It feels amazing. Unreal. This sort of thing doesn't happen. Not to me, anyway. The whole place is dead. The lights from the seafront are casting crazy shadows as we run off in all different directions, screaming, scattering stones about, spinning in circles before joining together again and flopping down, panting and exhausted.

Gemma takes one of the vodka bottles out of her bag. She passes it round and we all take a swig. Then we sit in silence, staring out into the darkness across the Channel.

six

"Tell you what we need to do," Dylan says, after we've been sitting for a while. "Build a fire."

He's not wrong. The night is mild, and there's no more than a gentle breeze blowing, but we're all shivering. The fact is, I didn't think this through. We're sitting on a beach at one in the morning in T-shirts. About ten minutes ago, a fox trotted past. It stopped to look at us and I swear I saw it shake its head.

Robbie snorts.

"How you going to start a fire then? Knock flints together?"

Gemma rummages in her bag again. She brings out a box of matches, shaking them like a single maraca.

"Thought these might come in handy," she says.

George puts his arm round her shoulders.

"That's my girl," he says.

Gemma giggles.

I look at George and chuckle to myself. He's turning into a bit of a smooth operator. It might have something to do with the amount of booze he's necked tonight.

I unwrap my arms from round my knees.

"Better get some things to burn then," I say.

I get to my feet and lead the way down to the

strand line, picking through the stuff left behind by the last high tide. Chunks of driftwood, fragments of yellow planks, broken pallets, bits of cork, netting, fishing wire, polystyrene. Anything flammable, we're having. Further up, we find some newspapers and fish and chip wrappers. The beach wasn't busy yesterday, but there's a lot of litter.

It doesn't take long to get a decent pile. While we keep foraging, Dylan tears up a newspaper and scrunches it into balls. Then he starts laying some of the bits and pieces we've gathered on the top. You can tell he was in the Cubs.

Pretty soon it's lighting-up time. We sit in a ring around Dylan's pyre. Dylan takes the box of matches from Gemma and strikes one, his face lit by a yellow glare. I'm hoping his cheap polyester Letchford shirt doesn't spontaneously combust. He cups the match in his hands and shoves it into the newspaper, moving it about, trying to spark it into life. To begin with there's only smoke, but then the first flames start licking their way through the wood and plastic.

Dylan looks up. He's beaming. We all cheer. Gemma passes the vodka round again, and then we sit back and watch the fire burn. It takes quite a while for it to get going. Everything's damp, hissing and spitting. There's an acrid smell in the air. From time to time moths flutter by to investigate, circling warily. One or two get too close and end up barbecued.

When the fire's crackling away nicely, I glance across at Steph. She's talking to Robbie, but I'm not so bothered this time. It doesn't feel like such a threat. Gemma and George are laughing quietly. They look good together. She's like a female version of him. Dylan's showing Nikita something on his phone. I glance at Steph again. This time she sees me looking and smiles. Not for the first time tonight, my heart leaps. I shuffle across the stones to sit next to her.

"Hopefully the fire should warm us up," I say. It's a bit of a dumb comment, but Steph's not put off.

"Yeah. And even if it doesn't, it's nice to watch isn't it? The flames make beautiful shapes."

"Mmm," I say. "I love fires."

Robbie looks a bit put out.

"I'm going to see if I can find anything else to burn," he says, standing up.

As I watch him go, I almost feel guilty. But not quite. Robbie's getting a taste of his own medicine. He's done it to me plenty of times.

Gemma hands me the vodka and I take a swig before passing it on to Steph. Then we get back to talking.

It's an unusual conversation. Not because we're talking about anything weird. It's just that after the ropey start, I'm finding myself telling her all types of things that I wouldn't normally come out with. Personal stuff. Stuff that I don't talk much to the lads about because they'd call me a ponce. Things I enjoy doing. Writing. Sketching. Watching old films.

It's not one-way traffic. I'm getting to know all about Steph. She plays the clarinet. She goes to gym classes. She likes old films too. Her dad separated from her mum when Steph was twelve and she isn't in touch with him any more. It's all getting pretty deep.

I decide to take a chance.

"Shall I tell you something embarrassing?"

Steph hooks a tendril of hair behind her ear. I notice her fingernails are painted black.

"What's that?" she asks.

"This sounds mad," I say. "But I reckon this is the first time I've had a proper conversation with a girl."

Steph nods, encouraging me to carry on. If what I'm saying *is* embarrassing, she's not going to make me feel bad about it.

"I mean, I've got a sister, Beth, who's two years older than me, and we get on alright. But we never actually talk about anything. We just mess around and try to get each other in trouble."

Steph nods again.

"What about girlfriends?" she asks.

"Well, you know. I've taken girls out to the cinema and for meals and shopping in the Ainsdale Centre in Letchford. And, don't get me wrong, it was okay. But I didn't really have a connection with any of them. I didn't feel like I could open up and be myself."

"And you do with me?"

My breath sticks in my throat. I'm going red. I'm hoping that, in the flickering light of the fire, it won't be too obvious.

"Er, yeah," I say. There's no going back. I've started talking about *feeling a connection* and *opening up*. I sound like one of those crappy Self Help books my mum reads. If Steph takes the piss now, that's the whole weekend ruined.

But she doesn't let me down.

"That's nice," she says, looking right at me. "I feel like I can talk to you too."

I get a surge of pride. That means something.

Steph pokes at the stones between her feet. She's thinking. Eventually she looks up.

"You told me something you're not proud of. I should do the same."

For a split second I go cold.

"You don't have to," I say.

There's an odd look on her face.

"You're going to think I'm making this up," she says. "But I'm not. It's awful. I don't know why I'm telling you, to be honest."

"You don't have to," I say again. I'm worried now. I don't want to have my illusions shattered.

Whatever it is, Steph's going to get it off her chest.

"Not last summer," she says, "the summer before, I got a police caution."

I'm amazed, but I try not to let it show.

"What for?"

Steph shakes her head in disbelief.

"Twoccing a car. Taking Without Owner's Consent. A BMW 3 Series. Wedged the door, then used the aerial to undo the locks. After that, I hotwired it. I drove round for a while, then I got pulled over. Don't know why I did it. Bored I suppose."

I let this information filter in. It's a bit of a surprise, but it's not as bad as it could have been.

Steph looks uncertain. There's something in her eyes. She's wondering how I'm going to react.

I try to lighten the mood.

"A Bimmer?" I say. "At least you nicked a good

motor. I mean it could have been a Skoda or some-thing."

Steph gives a half-smile, relieved but still unsure.

I should leave it there, but there's something that's nagging at me. I've got to ask.

"How did you know how to hotwire a car?"

Steph purses her lips.

"My dad was a bit of a wide boy. Knew about dodgy business. And he taught me quite a lot of it. That's why I know how to drive. He used to take me out on Sundays, round this disused airfield. It wasn't once or twice, it was loads of times. I got quite good. Dad had a BMW 3 Series, so it was no problem driving the one I twocced."

"He sounds like a cool bloke, your dad," I say.

Steph doesn't answer straight away. She runs her tongue along her teeth.

"There were some cool things about him. Some not so cool."

I nod my head slowly.

"So do you never see him at all nowadays?"

This time there's no hesitation.

"No. My mum and I don't have any contact with him any more. Probably for the best."

It sounds like Steph doesn't want to continue along this path. I move closer and squeeze her shoulder.

She looks at me.

"Do you think I'm really bad?" she asks.

"Yeah," I say. "Terrible."

But she knows I'm only joking.

I check my phone. I can hardly believe it. Half past two. While I've been talking to Steph, I've lost track of what's been going on. Not much, it seems. The fire is still burning. Dylan and Nikita are still chatting. Robbie's trying to build a stack of pebbles. And George is slumped into Gemma with a glazed look on his face.

The night's boozing is catching up with George. The vodka has sent him over the edge. We're onto the second bottle now and he's spannered. You'd have thought someone his size should be able to knock it back no problem at all, but he isn't much of a drinker. Usually, if we're having a few cans at someone's house, or a couple of bottles of cider on the park, George is the one who stays sober. Makes sure we don't do anything too stupid. Not tonight. I suppose he did try, earlier on when he rolled up with his pints of water. Strangely, he stopped worrying about keeping himself hydrated when the girls arrived. I notice he's got his hand on Gemma's knee. She doesn't seem to mind. I look at him and he dissolves into a fit of giggles.

"I'll tell you something," he says. His Brummie accent is twice as broad as normal. It happens when he's had a few.

"What's that George?"

George stops giggling. He looks deadly serious.

"Everyone likes a drink," he says. "But no-one likes a drunk."

I'm about to ask him what he's on about, but there's no point. He's doubled over, laughing so hard he's in danger of giving himself a hernia. I shake my head. It's the sort of thing his dad comes out with. He's a funny bloke, George's old man. Nice, but slightly odd. When George has finished laughing, he leans towards Nikita.

"I'll tell you something," he says. "Everyone likes a drink…"

Nikita cuts him off.

"Yeah, I know George. But no-one likes a drunk."

George looks disappointed. But he starts chortling again anyway.

Over the next hour we keep the fire going the best we can. We've used up the supplies of fuel on our part of the beach, so me and Steph head off over the groyne to scavenge on the next bit. Steph finds the blade of a kids' cricket bat, minus the handle, and I get a couple of fruit boxes that have floated in with the tide. They're a bit waterlogged, but the fire is roaring and they catch light no problem at all.

It's getting on for half past three. The vodka has gone. I've had a lot to drink. More than I've ever had before. But it's been over a long period. I'm a bit spaced out, but all in all, I don't feel too bad.

The sky is beginning to lighten. It's a charcoal grey colour, with a slight amber glow on the horizon. Dawn isn't far off. It's too early for seagulls to be flying, but there's one or two tatty specimens strutting about. The tide peaked a couple of hours ago and the sea's going back out again. Pebbles are rumbling backwards and forwards as the waves lap at the shore. I give the fire a poke and chuck on another piece of wood.

Everyone's quiet now. Tired and pissed. George hasn't come out with his *everyone likes a drink* line for ages. We need something to get us going. I've had another brainwave. I'm full of them tonight. I stand up and stretch.

"Come on," I say. "Let's go and paddle."

Robbie furrows his brow.

"You're kidding."

"No mate. I'm serious."

All eyes are on me now.

"Come on," I say again. "How many chances do you get to paddle in the sea at this time in the morning?"

Steph's the first one on her feet.

"I'm in."

Nikita gets up next.

"I'm with you," she says.

I'm impressed with Nikita. She's a tiny girl, not much more than five foot tall. She must only weigh eight stone. But she was knocking the alcohol back like a professional, and she's raring to go even at this hour of the morning.

Slowly but surely everyone else, even Robbie, starts peeling themselves up from the stones. As we crunch down the slope, the first sliver of the sun is appearing over to the left beyond the pier. About ten foot from the highest point the waves are reaching, we all sit down and start taking off our shoes and socks. Steph's toenails are painted black like her fingernails.

I roll up my trouser legs. This was my idea, so I've got to be brave. I've got to get on with it. I grab Steph's hand and we take the last few steps, pebbles digging into the soles of our bare feet. Holding onto each other, we splash into the freezing sea, screaming at the shock, wading out for a while then turning to look towards the beach.

The rest are holding back.

"In you come," I say, grinning. "The water's lovely."

George and Gemma are the first to follow, then Nikita, with Dylan and Robbie last to make a move. Finally all seven of us are up to our ankles. I try to take in all the details. The tiny lights along the pier. The sunrise. The stars. The beach. The stones rolling over my toes. It's another one of those moments in time. The ones you'll remember forever.

Thirty seconds of standing in the Channel at this time in the morning is more than long enough. My teeth are chattering and my feet are going numb. I lead the way back to the shore and drop down, drying my feet with one of my socks. I toss the other one across for Steph to use.

She smiles.

"Chris. What a gentleman you are. Who needs someone to lay a jacket over a puddle when you've got a pair of old socks?"

We both laugh.

When we've got ourselves sorted, we head for the fire. All the wood is gone now, and the flames have almost burnt themselves out. We sit and watch the embers dying down. It's getting lighter and lighter as the sun drags itself into the sky, a huge orange semicircle reflecting in the dark water. I can still see one or two stars, the moon is sinking down towards the sea, and there's a kind of mist rising up. It's a weird time. The night is fading, but it's not daytime yet.

I look at my watch. Nearly four o'clock. We've all gone quiet again. The truth is, it's time to go back to Wonderland. Everyone knows it. But nobody wants

75

to be the one that says it. Nobody wants to break the spell. In the end, Gemma speaks up.

"We need to think about getting some sleep," she says.

She's right. While people are struggling to their feet, I help Dylan stamp out what's left of the fire. When it looks like it's gone for good, we all trudge up to the prom.

We take it easy on the walk back. Away from the beach and the sound of the waves, it's deathly silent. Almost the whole of the sun is above the horizon now. The mist has lifted and the temperature is creeping upwards. The sky is clear and there's not a cloud in sight. Looking back along Whitbourne seafront, the pier is shining in the early morning light, gleaming white.

The seafront gradually disappears as we climb higher out of town. I'm walking alongside Steph. Every now and then my arm brushes against hers. I'm wondering how she would react if I grabbed hold of her hand. It would probably be a step too far. Too much, too soon. It's good enough just being with her.

Before long we're coming down the road with the tall trees. Two minutes later we're at the Wonderland entrance. We trace the bear paw prints through the foyer, cut across the courtyard then follow the path into Blue Zone.

For a few seconds everyone stands looking at one another, not knowing what to say. There's a strong feeling growing inside me, like a yearning. I'd do anything to be able to reach across to Steph and kiss her goodnight. But it's not going to happen. Not yet anyway.

"Shall we all get together tomorrow?" Nikita asks.

I'm in there like a shot.

"Yeah. That would be great."

Gemma nods.

"Okay," she says. "We're all going to need a lie-in in the morning, so why don't we agree to meet on the beach in the afternoon. Not too early. Say half past three at the bandstand?"

George gives a sleepy grin.

"Half three. It's a date."

I look at Steph.

"See you tomorrow then," I say.

Steph smiles.

"Yeah. See you tomorrow Chris. Sleep well."

My heart feels like it's going to explode.

The girls go off to their chalet and we walk the last few hundred metres to the caravan. As Robbie unlocks the door, I take a deep breath. The air tastes good. I just know tomorrow's going to be a brilliant day.

seven

I pop open one eye, then the other. Everything is blurred. Somewhere close by, I can hear a shrieking noise. My arms seem to be tied to my sides and I'm coated in sweat. Sunlight is streaming in through a window to my left, between a gap in some curtains. I stare at the brown fabric with chevron patterns on it. A jab of panic goes through my whole body. Where the hell am I?

The panic rises further. I suppose it's only a few seconds, but it feels a lot longer. I try to move my arms, rolling my eyes from side to side, looking for something familiar. Things are coming into focus now, but I don't recognise anything.

I'm about to start struggling and shouting when it all drops into place. A smile spreads across my face. False alarm. Seagulls are shrieking. I'm wrapped up in my sleeping bag. And I know those dodgy curtains. Robbie's caravan.

I blow out my cheeks and feel the anxiety ebbing away. My heartbeat is getting back to normal. I wriggle my arms out of my sleeping bag. Still lying down, I look across to the other bed. Robbie's not there. I reach over to the bedside cabinet and pick up my watch. Eleven-thirty. Shit. Half the day's already gone.

I prop myself up on my right elbow. Without

warning, the room starts spinning. A wave of sickness sweeps over me. I rub a hand across my face. My eyes make a squelching sound as I press my fingers into them. I groan and flop back onto my pillow. I can't believe it. I thought I was okay when I went to bed. But now I feel as rough as a badger's arse.

I lie completely still for a couple of minutes as the room gradually starts slowing down. I take a few breaths and wrestle myself out of my sleeping bag. I swing my feet onto the floor as carefully as I can, checking that it isn't going to move, then I stand up and stretch. My whole body seems to creak and my head is throbbing. It feels like someone has laid carpet on my teeth in the night.

I creep out of the bedroom shielding my eyes and holding onto the doorframe.

Robbie's at the kitchen sink in his boxers, washing last night's cider glasses and Pot Noodle forks.

"Morning," he says.

"Morning," I mumble.

I take one of Robbie's glasses and get myself a drink of water. It's not as cold as I'd like it to be, but I down it in one. It makes me feel a bit better, but not much.

Dylan and George haven't surfaced yet. I push open the door to their bedroom. The place reeks. Hours and hours of solid farting. I hold my nose and peer into the gloom. Nearest to me, Dylan's flat out, snoring like a warthog. On the far side, George is sitting hunched forward in his sleeping bag. He hears me come in, but he doesn't look up.

"Chris," he wails. "I'm dying."

I can't help laughing.

"Serves you right, you drunken slob."

My bladder feels the size of a football, so I head for the bathroom. Standing in front of the toilet, I try to concentrate on having a piss. It's taking a while, but I'm getting there. I look down. It's not good. Dark yellow, verging on orange.

When I'm finished, I run a hand through my hair and step up to the mirror. I pull down my lower left eyelid. Where my eye is supposed to be white, it's light pink. I look shattered and I need to get myself on track. I grab my sponge bag and step into the shower.

As the water splashes over my head, images from last night go round in my brain. Drinking cider. The Family Entertainment Centre. The hen party. The fighting. The beach. The stars. The fire. The girls. Standing in the sea. Did all that really happen? My stomach twists. Steph. Does she actually exist?

Thoughts of Steph fill my mind. The way she looks. The way she talks. The way she is. She's gorgeous, she's bright, and yet she's done something as mad as pinching a motor. How did that happen? It's like I've made her up. But I haven't. She's real. And I'll be seeing her again in a few hours.

I think of the things I said to her. Stuff I've never said to anyone else before. I'm expecting a hot rush of shame to swallow me up. Maybe I was being a tosser, running my mouth off because I'd had a few pints. But the rush of shame doesn't come. I've not got anything to feel embarrassed about. What I said I meant. It wasn't just the drink talking.

Ten minutes later, I'm out of the shower. I'm feeling a whole lot more human. I dry my hair and wrap the towel round my waist, sarong-style. I brush my teeth and I put a bit of wax in my fringe. Then I go back into the main part of the caravan.

George has made it out of the bedroom. He's taken two steps outside the door and collapsed on the floor. Now he's curled up in a foetal position, a puny white body in a pair of Paisley Y-fronts, whimpering like a baby.

I kneel down next to him.

"I know what you need, George mate," I say.

George keeps on whimpering.

Robbie's sitting over by the TV. I look at him and wink.

"You need the hair of the dog."

Robbie gets the bin bag from under the table and holds it open while I get out one of the empty bottles from last night. Ideally it would be vodka, but cider is the best I can manage. I unscrew the lid, then I poke the top under his nose. George starts writhing around, desperately trying not to inhale the smell of stale apples.

"Piss off," he howls. "Piss off."

I give him a few more wafts, but he's had enough. I leave him writhing and go back into my bedroom.

My clothes are lying in a crumpled pile between the beds. I pick up my jeans and have a look in the pockets, making sure I've not lost anything. My wallet and mobile are both there, along with a massive pile of coins. It's my change from a couple of trips to the bar in the Family Entertainment Centre. It looks like I've robbed a fruit machine. I tip all the coins onto the bed and count them, along with the notes in my wallet. All in, I spent about twenty-five quid last night. Not too bad. I put the coins on the bedside cabinet. Best not to take them down to the beach.

I slide open my phone, seeing if it's charged. The screen springs into life. *ONE MISSED MESSAGE. 09.30. MUM.* My heart almost stops. As I click the button to open the message, my hand is shaking. This could be the moment the whole weekend comes crashing down. But it isn't. It's only Mum saying good morning and asking if I'm okay.

Feeling guilty, I thumb in a reply. *Hi Mum. We all fine. C U 2moro nite. Luv Chris X.*

I chuck the phone on the bed and rummage in my bag for my camouflage shorts. I put them on and get a white T-shirt. A pair of trainer socks and my Etnies, mobile and wallet in my pockets, watch on my wrist, and I'm ready for the day.

It's nearly twelve o'clock now. Back in the living area, George has managed to scrape himself off the floor and he's sitting up at the far end under the big window next to Robbie, looking dazed. Dylan's finally stopped snoring and he's sitting on the edge of the bed, lifting his weights. I put the TV on. It's the news, but I can't be bothered to change channels.

George is squeezing the bridge of his nose between his thumb and forefinger. His complexion is usually quite pasty, but today there's a hint of green about him. He takes his hand away and looks at me.

"Oh God, Chris. What was I saying to Gemma on the beach last night?"

"Can't you remember?"

He puts his hand back across his eyes.

"Only bits of it," he says. "I was talking bollocks, trying to impress her. It was that vodka. It did my head in."

I start to laugh. Robbie's laughing too.

George grabs my arm.

"Don't Chris." There's anguish in his voice. "Oh God. I could have said anything."

I pull a stern expression.

"Well you know what they say George. Everyone likes a drink. But no-one likes a drunk."

George blushes. His face is red white and green now. All the colours of the Italian flag. He shuts his eyes.

"Oh God. I kept saying that. And I was putting my arm round Gemma, wasn't I?"

It's Robbie's turn to look serious.

"You did worse than that," he says.

George sits bolt upright.

"What? What did I do?"

Robbie shakes his head.

"It was terrible. You were all over her. Gemma had to ask me and Chris to calm you down."

George buries his face in his hands.

"Oh God. Oh God. I don't believe it. Are you joking?"

Robbie stays serious.

"That's right isn't it Chris?"

"Afraid so mate," I say. "You were getting a bit out of hand."

George slumps forward, moaning.

We leave him that way for a few seconds, then we can't keep it up any longer. I look at Robbie, Robbie looks at me and we both crack up.

George lifts his head. It takes him a while, but slowly he catches on. We're taking the piss.

"You bastards," he says.

I punch him on the shoulder.

"You daft twat. It looked like you and Gemma were getting on well."

"Do you reckon?"

"Yeah. For definite."

George still isn't convinced.

"And I didn't upset her, or make an idiot of myself?"

I shake my head.

George lets out a breath.

"Gemma," he says quietly. "Gemma Franks."

Saying Gemma's name a couple of times seems to perk him up. For the first time today, he looks more like his normal self. He stands and wanders over to the bathroom, leaving me and Robbie on our own.

After a while, it's getting obvious that neither of us is saying much. There's a slight atmosphere building. Robbie's got his nose out of joint because we both know he fancied his chances with Steph. Robbie's not used to rejection. In general he just has to flutter his eyelashes at girls and they come running. And because the girl he was after picked me, well, that's really needled him. It's made me feel pretty good though.

Robbie has a go at breaking the ice.

"Good night, last night."

I don't know if he's making a statement or asking a question.

"Yeah," I say, non-committal.

Robbie tries again.

"So what were you and Steph talking about then?"

I scratch my armpit.

"Not a lot. This and that." I'm keeping quiet. I know Robbie's fishing. Seeing if he's still in with a shout.

It sounds like George is in the shower now. I look back at the TV, pretending to be interested in the showjumping that's come on after the news. Robbie picks his phone off the table and starts fiddling with it.

Dylan's finished exercising. He comes out of the bedroom in a pair of grey jogging bottoms, pushing his fists together and flexing his pecs. He's like a whippet on steroids. Dylan's not the world's most perceptive bloke, but he senses there's something going on straight away.

"What's up with you two?" he asks.

"Nothing," I tell him.

Robbie keeps quiet.

Dylan narrows his eyes.

"Come on. You can tell your uncle Dylan."

"We're cool," Robbie says, still looking at his mobile.

Dylan's not buying it. There's a lop-sided grin twisting his mouth up on one side.

"You can't fool me. It's Steph, isn't it?"

For once in his life, Dylan's hit the nail on the head. But Robbie's not going to let him congratulate himself.

"I've got to be honest," he says. "I've got my eye on Nikita."

Dylan's face drops.

"Don't even joke about that. Anyway, Nikita

wouldn't be interested in a waster like you. She's too classy."

"Too classy?" I say. "How come you were buying condoms in the toilets then?"

Dylan sniffs.

"I didn't get them in the end." He looks like he's telling the truth.

I break into a smile. Robbie does too. It lifts some of the tension.

George takes about twenty minutes in the shower. When he's done, he looks ten times healthier than when he went in. Dylan's next up. He's fairly quick and so by half past twelve, it's just Robbie left needing to get ready. In true Robbie style, he seems to be taking ages. The showjumping is rambling on and on, but I still can't summon up the energy to find something else to watch.

As the time ticks towards one o'clock, Robbie comes out of the bathroom. He's showered and changed, but he doesn't look happy.

"What's up?" I ask.

He jabs his thumb over his shoulder.

"Which one of you left that huge crap in the toilet? It's the size of a piano leg."

George shakes his head.

"Not me. I had one up at the Family Entertainment Centre last night."

Robbie looks at me.

"You can count me out. I've not had one since we were in London yesterday."

Dylan's looking shifty. All eyes turn in his direction.

"Well, I suppose it must have been me," he says

eventually. "What do you want me to do about it? I flushed it twice, but it wouldn't go. I'm not putting my hand down there."

Robbie rolls his eyes.

"Well I'm not touching the thing. You'll have to see if you can get it moving with the bog brush. I told you last night. There's got to be absolutely no sign we've been here. And that means no skid marks."

Dylan grunts. I'm waiting for him to spit his dummy. He usually does. But today he just gets up and heads for the bathroom. Thirty seconds of scrubbing and he's back out again.

"Mission accomplished," he says.

I look at my watch. Five past one.

"Let's get shifting," I say. "We're supposed to be meeting the girls at three-thirty. At this rate we're not going to make it."

Robbie, Dylan and George go off to get the stuff they need. Two minutes later they're ready. George is fully recovered now and he's playing Mother Hen again. He's rolled up all our towels and put them in a bag to take down to the beach. We have a last look round, switching the TV off and making sure everything is how it should be. We get our sunglasses, then Robbie locks the caravan and we set off through Green Zone.

Everyone else at Wonderland has got a head start on us today. People are out and about, sunbathing, playing tennis, throwing Frisbees. Whitbourne is only down the hill, but it looks like most of the punters have opted for a day on the site. The kids from yesterday are still hanging around. They've got nothing to say to us now. They just nudge one another and giggle as we come past.

We're into Blue Zone. There's a bloke walking in our direction. Another late starter. He's got a bottle of milk in one hand and a copy of the *Daily Star* in the other. He's wearing a basketball vest and he's got little arms like pipecleaners, covered in tattoos. There's something familiar about him, but I can't put my finger on it. And then it hits me. The wispy facial hair. It's the fat woman's toyboy. As he comes past, he yawns and rubs the back of his neck. He looks knackered.

Robbie's seen him too.

"It must have been a hard night," he says.

I start to laugh, but the sound gets cut off. Because there's someone else heading our way. A short woman in a sun top with a towel wrapped round her head. Bev. She's twenty metres away and closing. I keep walking, staring down at the ground. At the last second I glance up. Bev is looking right at me. I'm about to stammer out an apology for buggering off last night, but I don't need to bother. There's not even a flicker of recognition in her eyes.

When she's gone past us, George squeezes my elbow.

"You left a big impression on her," he says.

We're coming to the end of Blue Zone, passing the swimming pool and the adventure playground. They're both full of kids. Robbie was right about Whitbourne livening up at the weekends. There's some movement in the Family Entertainment Centre, so we pop our heads round the door to have a look.

The place looks different in the daytime. The tables and chairs have been moved out of the middle of the floor and a bloke in a boiler suit is pushing a polisher round. Any broken glass and bloodstains are long gone. I didn't notice last night, but there are murals painted on the walls. Out-of-proportion Disney characters and a deformed Bart Simpson.

Two groups are up and running. Nearest to us, some old folks are sipping tea and complaining about the biscuit selection. Up at the far end, by the stage, it's some sort of playscheme. There's a vaguely Christian tone. The kids are standing in a circle singing a song about Jesus. Damaged, danger-ous-looking toys are strewn about everywhere. According to a sign propped up on an easel it's *Benny the Bear's Kidz Klub*. Sure enough Benny's there, dancing around. I wonder if it's the same bloke as last night in the suit.

We watch for a few more seconds then we nip across the courtyard and go into the foyer. Tonight's bill is scrawled onto the cardboard Benny's placard.

TONITE IS PARTY NITE!!!
FAMILY ENTERTAINMENT CENTRE
BINGO WITH VIC WHITLEY
AWARD-WINNING PSYCHIC COLIN WELLS
LINE DANCING LATE BAR

"I think we'll give that a miss," I say.

We push our way through the double doors into the car park and start the walk into town.

eight

"Oh man," George says. "I'm boiling."

We all are.

It's mega-hot this afternoon. The wind that was blowing yesterday has completely died away. There's a haze shimmering over Whitbourne as we come down towards the town. The sky is a perfect blue, criss-crossed with white vapour trails. The walk can't be more than a mile, but by the time we're at the lifeboat station I'm sweating like I've run the London Marathon.

The beach is much busier today. It looks like a few sunbathers have already been out way too long. Two lads are lying on Liverpool towels at the point where the pebbles start sloping down to the sea. One of them is so red, he's blending into his towel like a chameleon. His mate is almost purple. On the bowling greens, old blokes in white caps are wandering around puffing on pipes and on the crazy golf there's a long line of people putting their way across hump-back bridges, into clowns' mouths and under the sails of windmills.

As we pass along the seafront, my stomach is rumbling. We haven't eaten since about five o'clock last night. More than twenty hours.

"We going to get some food?" I ask.

There's a lot of head nodding.

"I saw a McDonald's in the town centre," George says.

"We'd be better off getting some junk from a pound shop," Dylan says. "Crisps and stuff. It'll save us money and it'll take less time. I want to get on the beach."

There's some more head nodding.

We're almost at the pier. There's an open-topped bus parked by the main entrance. *Discover Whitbourne* is stencilled on the side. They don't seem to have any passengers. We cut through the traffic and hang a left, up the road we came down yesterday. The cafes and ice cream shops are buzzing. Old ladies and young families are sitting at tables on the pavements eating scones and fish and chips and sundaes. We keep going, passing all the souvenir shops with their Whitbourne tea towels and racks of postcards, until we find what we're looking for. Poundtastic.

The shop is packed. The place smells of deodorant and sun tan lotion. Tinkly lift music is playing on the PA. I push my sunglasses up on my head and try to take it all in.

Poundtastic seems to stock every item under the sun. Down the first aisle the shelves are filled with jars of bath crystals, shell sculptures and CDs of Irish folk songs. It's pretty random. Up at the end, bottles of cheap perfume are mixed in with tins of rust paint. Down the second aisle it's plastic sandwich boxes and out-of-date annuals and dust-covered statuettes of the Queen Mother. *Limited Edition of 1000* it says on the boxes. They've got about nine hundred and ninety-eight left to sell.

Robbie sighs.

"Who decided we should come in here?" he asks.

I look at Dylan, expecting him to get the huff, but he just shrugs. He seems a lot calmer than usual today. He cleaned his crap out of the toilet without complaining, and now this. Must be something to do with Nikita.

Heading into the next aisle, we're finally getting somewhere. I grab a Family Value Selection of biscuits and a twelve pack of assorted crisps. Robbie tops this up with some chocolate chip flapjacks, a box of Wine Gums and a bag of Haribos, and Dylan adds some Fig Rolls and Boost bars. I get four big bottles of water and we join the end of a queue.

George checks out the rubbish we're holding and grimaces.

"We can't eat this. Put it back and we'll go into town and get something proper."

"Don't be soft," Dylan says. "We've got all the major food groups covered here."

George looks to me for support, but I'm not playing along. I'm so hungry I'd eat anything right now.

We're nearly at the front of the line. The geezer ahead of us is bagging up his bits and pieces. We put our dinner next to the till. The bloke behind the counter has got a big hairsprayed fringe and fingerless gloves. He's having a bad day by the looks of it. He puffs out his cheeks and pushes our shopping across the barcode reader.

"Nine pounds," he says, letting out a long breath.

I hand over a tenner and wait for my change.

Outside, we walk down to the seafront again, darting over the road by the pier and on towards the

92

bandstand. The prom is rammed. Dogs and kids are running riot and row after row of deckchairs is filled with old folks in sunhats. There's a massive group of English Language students, Spanish kids about our age with red and blue rucksacks, sitting along the low wall next to the ornamental flowerbeds. Some of the girls look a bit tasty.

We carry on up the prom until we get to the stretch of beach we were on last night. We cut across the stones and sit facing the sea. Lower down, the remains of our fire are still there, a black smudge in amongst the whites, reds, yellows and greys of the stones. Couples and families are spread out all around us, baking in the heat. Wobbling arses and orange peel thighs are everywhere. And that's just the blokes. Near the water there's a group of kids in Man Utd shirts. They're messing about, chucking stones at each other. It's going well until *ROONEY* hits *FLETCHER* right between the eyes and he crashes down in a heap. I shake my head and start unloading the food from the Poundtastic bags.

Fifteen minutes later I've worked my way through three bags of crisps, some custard creams, a big flap-jack bar, a Boost and a handful of sweets. I've washed it all down with a litre of spring water. My stomach isn't complaining any more. I made the mistake of chucking some bits of Fig Roll for two seagulls who were looking sorry for themselves. Now there's about forty of them wandering up and down, tilting their heads to one side seeing if they can cadge something else. They're out of luck.

George gets the towels out and we lie back, letting the food go down.

The day is getting hotter and hotter. Dylan swipes sweat from his forehead.

"Who's up for a swim?" he asks. "I need to cool off."

"Let's go for it," I say.

I sit up and start pulling my T-shirt over my head. Robbie and Dylan are stripping off too. I tuck my wallet, watch and phone under the corner of my towel.

"Lads," George says. "We've just finished eating. It would be dangerous to go swimming. We might get cramp."

I look at him, trying to work out if he's joking. He isn't.

Robbie jumps across onto George's towel and ruffles his hair.

"Come on Georgie Boy. Stop being so sensible. If you start drowning, I'll pull you out."

"And Dylan would love to give you the kiss of life," I say.

Dylan waggles his eyebrows.

George thinks about carrying on, but he can see that he's wasting his time.

"Well, don't say I didn't warn you," he says, taking his T-shirt off. It's another one only George could have bought. A Funny Man Shirt. Navy blue with *If Found Please Return To the Pub* across the front.

I'm ready for the water. The shorts I'm wearing are like George and Robbie's. They're designed for swimming. There's a pouch inside to rest your bits in. Dylan's in a pair of cut-off jeans.

"You're not going in the sea in those are you?" I ask.

Dylan shakes his head. He starts pulling the jeans

down his legs. Underneath, he's wearing a tiny pair of black Speedos.

Robbie's copped a look at them. He's laughing his head off.

"What the hell are they?" he splutters.

"They're proper budgie-smugglers," I say.

Dylan throws his jeans onto his towel and gets up, adjusting his package.

"These are what real swimmers wear. You never see people in the Olympics in Bermuda shorts do you? And I don't know about budgie-smugglers. Pigeon-smugglers maybe."

George smirks.

"Hummingbird, more like."

Dylan readjusts his parts.

"Anyway. Are we having a swim or are you girls going to spend the afternoon looking at my groin?"

We all stand up. The tide is right in and lots of people are already paddling. Overweight men and women in badly-fitting swimwear, kids with arm-bands. On the horizon I can see an oil tanker inching its way along. Heading down the beach, we come past the strand line where we hunted for firewood last night. It's a grim sight in the daylight. There's a bottle of Yop, some feathers, a dead flatfish, three beer cans and a used condom.

Dylan tuts.

"You reckon this beach has got a Blue Flag?"

"Doubt it," Robbie says. "They get some strange things washed up. One year when I was a kid, they had a Minke Whale. Poor bastard took a wrong turn out in the ocean and wound up here. It was on the news. They tried to drag it back into the sea, but the tractor got stuck."

"Shit," I say. "What a way to go. Suffocated in Whitbourne."

We're at the edge of the water now and we wade in, up to our waists. It's not much warmer than it was last night. In this heat, that's a good thing. Dylan's the first to put his head under, diving through a wave and freestyling out to the end of the groynes. I'm next, and pretty soon we're all bobbing around, splashing and shouting.

I take a lungful of air and go underwater to de-bag George. I nearly get his shorts right off, but he grabs hold of them when they're round his ankles. As I'm coming up to the surface, Robbie ducks me back in, and then all three of us team up on Dylan. I get his legs, George and Robbie get his arms and we manage to lift him up out of the water and sling him in. He doesn't mind though.

I swim straight out, cutting across the course of an old bloke in a rubber cap who's thrashing away at the water like a blindfolded drunk fighting. Soon I'm quite a long way from shore. I stop and tread water, looking across at the pier. It's an assortment of white-painted buildings, stretched out along a wooden platform. There's a big thing like a hall near the front, another up at the end. In between there are all sorts of little huts and shacks. It's like a shantytown on spindly metal legs.

I turn ninety degrees and look at the beach. It looks different from here. A patchwork of colours and shapes. There's not many people this far out. Just a couple of lads on a lilo. It's lonely and quiet. I find myself thinking about my mum and dad. What would they say if they could see me now?

I'm starting to get cold, so I scull back across to Robbie.

"Going back to the towels mate," I say.

Back on the stones I dry myself off, put my watch on and check that my mobile and wallet are where I left them. The seagulls have cleared off. I lay my towel down again, turning it round to track the sun in the sky. Over to the right, the old bloke in the rubber cap is still swimming. He's moved onto breaststroke. He looks like one of those wind-up frog bath toys. I watch him for a while until Robbie, George and Dylan make their way up the slope.

"Enjoy that?" I ask.

"Yeah yeah yeah," Robbie says, bending forward and swishing his hair from side to side like one of those old English sheepdogs, sending little beads of water flying everywhere.

George turns his towel round so it's facing the same way as mine, and Dylan fiddles with his Speedos, getting his package sorted out.

"We didn't get cramp then, George," I say.

George smoothes his hair down.

"You can never be too careful."

I put my sunglasses on and check my watch. Nearly ten to three. I've tried not to think about Steph for the last couple of hours. But I'm thinking about her now. We're supposed to be meeting the girls in forty minutes. I look out to sea again. There's no sign of the old bloke any more. A couple of lifeguards on the next beach along are exchanging worried glances.

We all lie back to get some sun. It's really beating

down. Half an hour passes slowly. I can feel the tops of my feet starting to burn, so I sit up and put my trainers and socks on. I'm not in the mood for sunbathing anyway. I'm itching to see Steph again. It's a weird sensation. Something totally new. When we set off from Letchford yesterday, I never thought anything like this would happen. I thought we were coming down here to piss about and have a bit of fun.

"Better get ourselves down to the bandstand," I say, sticking my top back on.

Robbie and George start getting their shirts on. Dylan's leaving his off. To impress Nikita, I suppose.

I lob a pebble at him and laugh.

"Get some clothes on, you buff twat."

Dylan looks pleased with himself.

"If you had abs and lats like this Chris, you'd live your life topless."

George rolls up our towels and puts them in his bag. Robbie grabs the Poundtastic carriers with our rubbish in, and we head up the beach.

Back on the prom the crowds have thinned out. It's getting too hot. A lot of the oldies have gone back to their hotels for a while, and the Spanish kids with rucksacks have separated into groups sitting on different parts of the beach. The two sunburnt Scousers we saw earlier are sitting in the shade of an overhanging yukka. They're dabbing sunblock on one another, but it's too little, too late. They're both purple now.

It's not far to the bandstand. The sun is bouncing off the blue domed roof. There's nothing on at the moment, but two blokes are putting out the deckchairs ready for later. A banner hanging across the front of the stage is advertising tonight's show.

SATURDAY LIVE AT 8.00
THE WHITBOURNE CONCERT ENSEMBLE
CLASSICAL FAVOURITES
THE 1812 OVERTURE AND
FIREWORK DISPLAY

Robbie looks at the banner.

"They've had that same show on every Saturday night since I was a kid."

"Must be a bit of a crowd-pleaser," George says.

"Dunno about that. Fireworks at the end are brilliant though."

We sit on the wall by the flowerbeds and wait. Butterflies and bees are skittering about behind us. I have another glance at my watch. Twenty-five past three. As I look up again, I see the girls walking down towards us. They're all ready for the beach in flip-flops and sunglasses. Steph's leading the way. My heart leaps. It feels like it's stuck in my throat.

As I'm trying to get my emotions straightened out, a nasty chain of thought starts off in my head. What if Steph's funny with me today? What if, without the alcohol and the night-time, she thinks I'm a bit of a nob? I can't believe I didn't put her number in my mobile. I could have texted her today. Then I'd know how things were going to be. My heart sinks. All that stuff I said to her. Earlier on I convinced myself it was nothing to be ashamed of. Now I'm not so sure.

The girls have seen us. They're fifty metres off

and closing. The next few seconds are going to be vital. I hold my breath. But then Steph starts to wave. She's smiling. Happy to see us. Happy to see me. It's going to be okay.

"How are you doing, boys?" Nikita asks.

"Not bad," Dylan says, standing as tall as he can, making sure his six-pack is on show.

Robbie puts his arm round Dylan. He looks at Nikita and grins.

"Don't you love that washboard physique?"

Nikita giggles, while Dylan goes into a bodybuilding pose.

I look at him and wonder if he had the doubts in his mind that I had. Not likely, knowing Dylan. But as I glance at George, I can see that he's had precisely the same thoughts as me flickering through his head. He really *did* make a dick of himself last night. Gemma seems fine though, and the relief is written all over George's face.

Steph sits down next to me. She's even more gorgeous in the daylight. For the first time, I see her eyes are light green. There's a spark to them that makes her look like she's just about to burst out laughing. Her hair is tied up again, shining in the sun. She's still wearing the black nail varnish she had on last night. It's slightly chipped in places, but it looks cool.

"Having a good day?" she asks.

"I am now," I say, smiling.

nine

The bit of beach nearest the bandstand is heaving, so we climb over the groyne to the next stretch of stones. With me and Steph out front, we head for a big patch of open space right in the middle. There's plenty of room for all seven of us to spread out for some hardcore sun-worship.

George rummages in his bag for our towels and tosses them to us. I notice that Gemma's doing the same thing for the girls. Last night I had her down as George in a skirt. I was right.

Gemma's bag is huge. The girls have come better prepared than us. They've not only got towels, they've got thin bamboo mats to lie on, little bolster pillows, loads of bottled drinks and enough sun tan cream to keep them going for months.

It's not long before we've all got ourselves sorted. There's a long row of us. Me, Steph, Gemma, George, Robbie, Dylan and Nikita. Towels have been smoothed out, sharp stones have been removed and we're almost ready for the burn. I take off my shoes and socks then, a bit self-consciously, pull my T-shirt up over my head. My physique isn't much in comparison with Dylan's, but I reckon Steph looks for something more in a bloke than big biceps. The thing is, she's peering at me and shaking her head.

I sit upright, pulling my stomach in.

"How long have you been in the sun today?" Steph asks.

"Dunno. Couple of hours I suppose."

"I bet you haven't had sunscreen on have you?"

"Er, no," I say.

Steph shakes her head again.

"Typical lad. You're going bright pink."

I pull a face. I was just laughing about those Scousers being sunburnt.

"Here," Steph says. "Put this on."

She passes me some Factor 15. I squirt a bit into my hand and rub it across my chest, my stomach and the front of my legs. It smells nice. Like coconut. I hand the bottle back.

"You need to put it all over," she says. "Lie on your front and I'll cover the rest of you up."

I can't believe my luck. I do as she says, fighting against the urge to let a stupid grin spread across my face as I feel her kneading my shoulder blades and moving in circles on her way down to the top of my shorts.

"All done," she says eventually.

I roll over.

"Thanks," I say.

Steph starts taking off her shirt and shorts. I try not to stare but it's difficult. She looks amazing. Nikita and Gemma look good too, Nikita in a green tankini and Gemma in one of those tan-through swimsuits like my mum wears, but Steph's something else. She's in a red bikini with white polkadots. Her skin is golden, her legs are smooth and toned. She slaps sun cream across her front, gently working it in, then she lies down face first on her towel.

"Right," she says matter-of-factly. "I need my back doing."

My heart doesn't so much leap, as jump right out of my chest and bounce off into the centre of Whitbourne. But I've got to get a grip on myself.

"Yeah," I say, as casual as possible. "No problem."

I pick up the sun lotion and do my best not to catch Robbie's eye as he stares at me open-mouthed. I smear some of the cream between my palms and slowly massage it into Steph's skin. I run my hands across her back, down her sides, over her hips. I wish I could carry on, but it would be too obvious what I was up to. I click the cap back on the bottle and hand it to her, then I stretch out to soak up some sun.

I do ten minutes on my front, then turn over for ten minutes on my back. Soon I'm on the verge of dozing off. The warmth, the gentle crashing of the waves, the tiredness from last night, the remnants of my hangover. They're all tipping me over the edge. I've been totally out of it for a while when Steph nudges me in the side.

"What's up?" I ask, still half-asleep.

Steph looks concerned. She gestures up the beach.

"There's something happening over there."

I push myself onto my elbow and squint my eyes in the direction she's pointing. Up to the right there's a group of the Spanish kids we saw earlier, two boys and two girls. Only they're not alone. They've been joined by what looks like local lads. Six of them. The locals are sitting with their backs to us, but it's not too difficult to see what's going on. A bit of good old-fashioned sexual harassment. A flavour of England that probably wasn't in the brochure.

The Spanish girls are getting flustered. One of the lads looks scared, but the other one isn't taking any crap. He's a little bloke, skinny with floppy black hair and a bumfluff moustache, but he's standing up, waving his arms around.

"Piss off," he's saying. "Piss off. Wankers."

I'm impressed. He's obviously been learning something useful at the Language school. The problem is, the lads aren't pissing off.

I sit up and get my sunglasses. Quite a few people have clocked what's going on. Families are picking up their stuff and moving away in case things get nasty. George is still flat out, but Robbie and Dylan are on the alert.

Robbie looks across at me.

"Better keep an eye on this," he says. "Six on two isn't exactly a fair contest. There's no other Spanish kids to help them out."

I nod. I start putting my trainers and socks on, just in case.

The other Spanish lad is joining in the verbals now. He's taller than his mate but if anything he's even skinnier. His grey hoody is hanging off him. One by one, the locals are getting to their feet. The two Spanish girls look close to tears. It's about to kick off.

Robbie and Dylan have got their shoes on. Robbie pokes George in the ribs. He finally realises what's occurring. He puts his shoes on too.

I stand up.

"Come on. We need to go and have a word."

Earlier, Steph was looking concerned. Now there's fear in her eyes. It's the way she looked last night, when the fighting started in the Family Entertainment Centre.

"Chris, be careful," she says.

I don't say anything. I just nod.

Up the beach, things are reaching a critical point. As the four of us crunch across the stones I'm completely psyched up. I don't know what we're going to do. But we can't sit around sunbathing while some kids get a shoeing.

The Spanish lads have seen us coming. They both look terrified. For all they know, the six kids they thought they were dealing with has become ten. But we're here to even up the numbers. If it gets physical, it's six-on-six.

The first of the local mob has seen us coming. He's a little shortarse in a red cap with a face like pizza topping. I know him from somewhere. He nudges the big bloke next to him. And when he turns round, everything clicks. Gelled hair. Brown and cream Nikes. Tattoo on his neck. Kirkie.

"Well, well," Kirkie says. "Look who it is."

His whole gang is catching on. It's like a chain reaction. They've forgotten all about the Spanish lot.

The kid with the head shaped like a lightbulb leers at us. He's still wearing his box-fresh fake Timberlands. He's got a black eye since I last saw him, a big comedy shiner like something you'd see on *Tom and Jerry*.

"The out of towners," he grunts. He runs out of inspiration after that.

For a few seconds we all stand looking at each

other. In the end it's George who speaks up.

"Now come on," he says, chewing at his lip. "Lets all stop messing. There's no need for any aggro."

Kirkie's mate in the red cap takes a couple of steps forward. He seems to have got the wrong end of the stick.

"You want aggro?" he says. "I'll give you some aggro, boy."

I look at him and sigh. Watching him having a pop at George is like watching a Chihuahua biting the ankles of a Great Dane. But I'm getting a sinking feeling. We shouldn't have got into this.

A thin kid in a cheap white anorak with red tartan across the shoulders starts staring me out. His bottom jaw is wider than the top of his head. His ginger hair is shaved round the sides and spiked on top. The ends are frosted blond. He's got his phone in his hand, pointing it round, taking the whole scene in. Something to post on YouTube.

Lightbulb Head glares at me and Robbie.

"Were you cheeky twats taking the piss yesterday?"

I wish he hadn't asked that. I feel like laughing again. I glance across at Robbie. I can see he's thinking along similar lines.

"Look," I say. "This doesn't have to get out of hand. Let's all get on with our own business, yeah?" Even as I'm saying the words, I know how lame they sound.

A fat kid with sticky-out teeth, the one who had a fag behind his ear yesterday, gets involved.

"Kirkie told you. You come to Whitbourne, you pay for the privilege. We're taxing you."

The rest of the mob starts laughing. They seem to be taking it in turns to have a go. It's like a shit boy-band all doing their solo spot. Kirkie's standing back and watching.

The next member is stepping up. He looks a bit like a bulldog. He's broader than he is tall, in baggy shorts and a vest, topped off by a woolly hat with earflaps. He's got phoney tribal tattoos on both shoulders. Something tells me he's the token bitch of the bunch. He's even more badly-dressed than the others, and he's got the saddest pair of trainers you've ever seen. Lime green Adidas. The kind they have on the sale rack outside JJB Sports.

"So come on. Wallets at the ready. It's taxation time." For some reason he's got a Jamaican twang to his voice. Robbie's mum's parents were born in Jamaica, but their accents aren't as broad as that. When he's finished, he looks up at Kirkie for approval, but he's getting blanked.

Robbie shakes his head.

"We all know that's not happening."

It's a proper standoff. The Spanish kid in the hoody tries to butt in, but no-one's listening. My thoughts are all over the place. I don't know what's coming next. I've got no idea if I'm any good at fighting. I've never had to find out. Sweat is running down my back. It's got nothing to do with the temperature. I start to wish I wasn't wearing my sunglasses. They cost me twenty-five quid from Top Man, and I could see them getting smashed here.

I'm not sure why, but my mind has started acting like a sponge, soaking up pointless details. A Union Jack and an EU flag fluttering on the roof of The

Glenroy Hotel. A cloud that looks a bit like a dolphin. Two dogs up on the prom who've taken time out from charging around to hump each other in the flowerbeds while a couple of old ladies try to prise them apart with their walking sticks.

Kirkie hauls the waistband of his jeans up over the top of his pants. Like the last time, he's let his lieutenants have their go and watched them get nowhere. He sucks air in through his teeth and gets ready to take the initiative.

"Right," he says. "Playtime's done, you get me? You turn over your money and your phones or someone's going to get hurt."

This isn't good. I swallow and sneak a peek back to where the girls are sitting. Gemma and Nikita have got their hands over their mouths. Steph's covering her eyes. In a funny way I'm glad. She won't see if I end up getting my head kicked in. I think about something George said yesterday. Drinking dinner through a straw. Not a nice image. The kid with the mobile has moved round to get a different angle.

So far Dylan's kept his mouth shut. It's not like him. It's a bit ominous. I picture him grabbing his balls in the street yesterday. I picture him shadowboxing in the caravan. I remember the things he said. Kirkie's lot were pussies. Slobs. We could take 'em. Any minute now, I'm expecting him to come out with something really aggressive. The thing that will finally light the blue touch paper. I'm wrong.

"Everyone needs to settle down," he says, cool and collected. "Baywatch is here."

At first I don't get what he's talking about. But

then I see. Two lifeguards, big dudes, surfer's haircuts, yellow T-shirts and red shorts, are on their
way over.

Lightbulb Head tugs at Kirkie's sleeve.

"Kirkie," he says.

Confusion flickers across Kirkie's face.

The lifeguards have arrived. They look round at
all of us, getting a handle on what's up. It isn't hard.
Neither of them says anything. They don't need to.

Kirkie's up to speed now. He knows it's Game
Over. He snorts phlegm up his nose and spits it
down onto the pebbles.

"We're out of here," he says.

He turns and leads his crew back up the beach to
the prom. When they get there, Lightbulb Head
spins round to look at us. He jabs two fingers
towards his eyes, then points them at me. *I'm
Watching You.* Next he draws his thumb across his
throat. *You're Dead.*

I look at Robbie and grin. Tension is bubbling out
of me.

"Someone's good at sign language," I say.

The biggest lifeguard looks at me and raises his
eyebrows.

"Everyone okay here?"

I give him the thumbs up.

He nods to his mate and they start heading back
to the strip of beach they came from. The Spanish
kids are leaving too. I don't blame them. They're
probably going off to find the rest of their group.
Safety in numbers. The lad with the moustache
looks at me and lifts his hand. I give him the same
signal back. At least he knows that not all English

people are wankers.

George is shaking his head and Dylan's standing with his hands on his hips. They both look a bit wired, but I'm feeling pretty good. Like a caveman who's just helped to see off another tribe. I high-five Robbie and we wander back to the girls.

Gemma and George start talking quietly. Dylan and Nikita do the same. I wink at Steph, but she's not looking amused. She's upset. She's trying to smile, but it's forced. Her mouth is turning up at the corners, but there's nothing registering in her eyes. The spark has gone.

Robbie sets off down the beach for a swim. I feel like joining him, to work off some of the adrenaline that's still coursing through me, but I can't leave Steph. I notice her hands are trembling.

I touch her arm.

"I'm sorry Steph. That wasn't very nice. But I couldn't just sit here."

Steph shakes her head.

"No. You did the right thing. But it seemed like those lads knew you. How come?"

I brush a stone off my towel.

"We had a bit of a run-in with them yesterday. Wasn't anything serious."

Steph's still trembling.

"You're not keen on stuff like that, are you?" I say.

She winces.

"I've seen enough violence to last me a lifetime. I know the damage it can do."

I nod, partly to show that I understand, partly to let her know she can talk to me about it if she wants to. I get the impression that her dad's something to do with the violence she's seen.

Steph stays quiet. She lies back on her towel and closes her eyes.

I take a deep breath and settle down on my front, keeping my eyes open in case anything dodgy starts developing. It seems okay though. Kirkie and his boys have gone. The whole stretch of beach is more or less empty now. It should be nice, having the place to ourselves, but it's not. It's like a damper's been put on the whole afternoon. Nobody's heart is in it any more.

I look at Steph again. I want to say something to her, but I can't think what. I've not known her for long, but she comes across as a tough kid. Not someone who'd want sympathy. But now she seems so fragile. I feel a big twinge. Some kind of emotion twisting my guts. I can't explain it, and I'd never say it out loud. At least not when the lads were listening. But maybe this is what love feels like.

ten

It's around five o'clock when we pack up and start the hike up the hill out of town. By half past we're coming past the barbed wire and crossing the car park at Wonderland.

Back in the foyer, there's been a late change to the bill at the Family Entertainment Centre. On Benny's placard, a red line has been drawn through *AWARD-WINNING PSYCHIC COLIN WELLS*. *Cancelled due to unforeseen circumstances* is scribbled underneath.

I look at Dylan.

"Colin's powers are failing him."

Dylan shrugs.

"Nah," he says. "He'd foreseen how crap this place is."

We carry on into the courtyard. Wherever I look, sunburnt people are wandering in a daze, going in and out of the shops. Red noses and shoulders are everywhere. I'm glad Steph got me to put sun cream on.

"Right then," Gemma says. "We're going back to the chalet to get something to eat, but we'll meet up later, yeah?"

"What time are we going to say?" George asks.

The girls look at each other. Nikita speaks up.

"Shall we call it eight?"

"Eight's fine," Dylan says. "We can go back into town, see what it's like at night."

Nikita nods.

"That would be great," she says.

George scratches his head.

"So are you going to come to us, or are we going to come to you?"

"You come to us," Gemma says. "We're Blue 29. It's along the row nearest the shops. Dead easy to find."

It sounds like everything is settled. Steph's been quiet since we left the beach. The whole thing with Kirkie and Co has really got to her.

"See you in a couple of hours then Steph," I say, trying to cheer her up.

It does the trick. The twinkle is back in her eyes.

"Yeah," she says, smiling. "Look forward to it."

The girls start off for their chalet, leaving us standing in the courtyard. The night's entertainment is sorted out so we need to think about food.

"What do you reckon then?" I ask. "Pot Noodles, crisps and Jaffa Cakes again?"

George isn't pleased.

"You're joking. We've not had anything decent to eat since we left Letchford. What about a Chinese? I know it isn't the healthiest, but at least it's something that's been cooked. Not just something we've tipped boiling water into."

I look across at Happy Valley. There's still a patch of puke on the pavement outside, and two seagulls are fighting over the chunky bits. But there's an *Open* sign in the window and the smell of sweet and sour is in the air.

"It's not a bad idea," I say.

Dylan and Robbie nod their heads.

"Right then," George says, pleased. "Chinese it is."

It's hot inside Happy Valley. Apart from us, only two other people are in the place. A geeky kid with glasses and a Monty Python T-shirt, and a twitchy bloke in a blue jogging suit with a picture of a trainer stitched to the leg. It's the outfit I saw on a washing line last night. The worst one I've ever seen. It looks even more terrible on.

The sweet and sour smell is much stronger in here. I'm absolutely starving. I take a couple of menus and we make for a bench next to the fish tank in the corner. Neon Tetras swim in and out of a sunken galleon while we decide on our meals. I'm having Peking Chicken. Robbie's having Cantonese Roast Pork. George opts for Shrimp and Beansprouts. Dylan rounds things off with a House Special Chop Suey. Four portions of Egg Fried Rice and we're sorted.

I go across to place the orders with the old Chinese chap behind the counter. It comes to twenty-eight quid. I pay up, sit back down by the fish tank and watch the TV bolted to the wall.

Ten minutes later our food turns up in two brown paper carrier bags. We head out and go into the Supermarket. Food's taken care of. It's time to get something to wash it down with.

Robbie disappears off to the back of the shop and comes back with two four-packs of Fosters.

"This should do the trick," he says.

"Too right." I'm glad he's gone for lager. I didn't fancy another session on the White Thunderbolt.

114

We're almost running on the way back to the caravan. We're all gagging for food. Robbie yanks the door open and goes into the kitchen cupboards to get plates and forks.

Sitting at the low table, I start dishing up, tipping Egg Fried Rice out of plastic tubs and plonking the main courses on top. George puts the TV on, flicking over to *Britain's Next Big Thing*. Dylan passes the cans of beer round and we crack them open.

It doesn't take me long to scoff my dinner down. Five minutes tops. I slide the plate onto the table and slouch back in my seat. I take a long swig of Fosters.

"That was cracking," I say.

There's a few grunts in agreement.

On *Britain's Next Big Thing* a young lad with ironed hair is yowling his way through a power ballad. He's straining for the high notes, twisting his features so it looks like he's trying to shit a pineapple.

Everyone's finished their dinners. I look at George. This meal was his idea, so I'm expecting him to be happy now. He's not though. There's a haunted expression on his face.

"What's the matter?" I ask.

George lines up his cutlery.

"I've got a bad feeling about tonight," he says.

"Why's that then? Because of that aggro on the beach with Kirkie's lot?"

George nods. He seemed alright earlier on, but perhaps that was because the girls were there. Now he looks rattled.

"Come on mate," I say. "It's going to be fine. A

night to remember. On the beach, that was sod-all. A bit of handbags."

"I'm not so sure. We keep on bumping into those idiots. A town this size, it's hard not to. If we see them again there's going to be big trouble. We'd be better off staying here."

"George. We can't go round to the girls' chalet and say 'Sorry ladies. Tonight's off.' We'd look like tossers. I mean, you didn't say anything when the whole thing was getting organised."

Dylan's keeping out of it, but Robbie's joining in.

"Look. No way are we staying cooped up in this place. You know what's on down at the Family Entertainment Centre. Bingo and line dancing. Even the psychic's bailed out. I want to go into town, Chris does and Dylan does. Trust me. It's going to be okay."

George bites his bottom lip. He's outnumbered and he knows it.

"Well, it's your call. But I've got a bad feeling about it. There's going to be some bother. It's like Instant Karma. Punishment for lying to our mums and dads."

Robbie pokes his finger in his ear and wiggles it about.

"Instant Karma?" there's disbelief in his voice. "You've not gone Buddhist on us have you?"

George shrugs.

We spend the next hour staring at the TV, letting our food go down. It's the decision stage on *Britain's Next Big Thing*. We're with the young lad with the ironed hair again. He's mooching moodily around a sunlit garden in a vest and flip-flops, waiting to learn his fate. I'm not paying much attention, but it doesn't look positive. He's blubbering on the shoulder of the presenter's shiny suit. Seven o'clock is coming around.

I finish my can and push myself upright.

"I'm going to make a start in the bathroom," I say.

There are no objections.

In the bathroom I sit on the toilet. I've eaten some serious junk over the last twenty-four hours, and judging from the sounds underneath me, my body is letting me know it doesn't approve. I hardly dare look into the bowl when I'm done, but out of curiosity, I take a peek. It's not a pretty sight. Pale and floaty. Not the bowel movement of a healthy man. I flush it away and spray a bit of George's deodorant round to mask the smell.

It's time to get ready. I have a quick rinse in the shower, getting all the dried sea salt out of my hair. I can taste it as it runs down my face. Afterwards I brush my teeth, spray my pits and work my way through my going-out checklist.

When I'm finished, George makes for the shower and I go into the bedroom, wrapped in my towel. I get clean socks and boxers and the jeans I wore on the trip down. I'm running a bit short of clothes I haven't already used this weekend, but I'm pleased to see I packed my turquoise polo shirt.

I stick on my Etnies, transfer my wallet and mobile into my jeans and wrap my watch round my wrist. When I've stuffed my pile of change into my pockets, I just need to get my bangles from the bedside cabinet where I dumped them last night, and I'm ready to roll. A quick glimpse in the mirror in

George and Dylan's bedroom confirms what I'd thought. I'm looking good.

Back in the living area I crack open my second can. *Britain's Next Big Thing* is still in full flow. It's been on for two hours now, and shows no signs of ending any time soon. I'd got it all wrong about the lad who was on earlier. He's not been eliminated. He's through to sing in the live part of the show. It's Big Band Night and he's dressed up in a dinner jacket complete with loosened bowtie, murdering a Frank Sinatra song.

Dylan's in the bathroom now. With George off getting changed, it's just me and Robbie watching TV.

Robbie takes a mouthful of beer and looks me in the eye.

"So you going to go for it with Steph tonight?" he asks.

I cough, caught off-guard.

"Dunno mate. Reckon I should?"

Robbie nods.

"Yeah yeah yeah."

I wipe condensation off the side of my can.

"D'you really think she's into me?"

Robbie pulls an exasperated face.

"She's mad for you," he says. "You've done all the negotiation. It's time to seal the deal."

I know he's right. But something is still nagging away in the back of my brain.

"I thought you fancied her," I say.

Robbie sighs.

"I did. But she wasn't interested. She likes you. Must be something wrong with her."

I laugh.

"No hard feelings?"

"Don't be a cock," Robbie says. "It's not your fault she's got no taste."

I look at him and smile. Robbie can be a bit of an arse, but it's at times like this that I remember why he's my best mate.

George is coming out of the bedroom. It looks like he's finally got the lads' night out clobber situation cracked. He's in a black and white striped T-shirt and dark blue jeans. His hair's still ropey, but he looks sixteen, not sixty. He sits down next to us, making a start on can number two.

It's twenty-five to eight. Dylan seems to be taking a lot longer than usual in the shower tonight, so I go to find out what he's up to.

It's steamy in the bathroom, but I have no difficulty seeing Dylan. He's standing in front of the mirror. And he's got my bottle of moisturiser in his hand.

"Oh. Alright Chris?" he says. There's a guilty look on his face.

"What are you up to?" I ask.

He holds up the moisturiser.

"Er, I wanted to have a go with this. Don't mind do you?"

I smirk. Dylan's discovered the joys of men's grooming.

"Help yourself," I say. "Nikita likes a well-turned-out man, does she?"

Dylan's got his composure back.

"Yeah. Something like that."

I laugh and leave him to it.

Five more minutes and Dylan's winding up his

male model routine. He strolls into the bedroom looking very happy with himself. He's fully moisturised, he's put a bit of my wax in his hair and he's splashed himself in aftershave.

Robbie wolf-whistles him.

"You'll be shaving your bollocks next, you tart."

Dylan grins.

"I'm not a tart," he says. "I'm a metrosexual."

Because Dylan's had such a session with the beauty products, Robbie's up against it. He doesn't let us down though. He's showered and dressed in fifteen minutes flat. And his standards haven't slipped. He's looking as sharp as always, in black jeans and a grey V-neck T-shirt.

It's five to eight. Dylan's been sitting with me and George for the last few minutes, but he nips back into the bathroom to check himself out one more time. He's upped his style game all-round. There's no football top and baggy trousers tonight. It's straight-cut jeans and a check shirt with a button-down collar. On the TV, the lad on *Britain's Next Big Thing* is in tears again. And this time it definitely isn't good news. He's been voted off.

"Poor sod," George says. "After all that."

I laugh.

"Never mind. He's been on an incredible journey."

George finishes his can and shoves it into the bin bag. He sits back and burps loudly. Not so long ago, he had the look of a condemned man about him. Not any more. Now he's completely chilled-out and ready for the night ahead. The calming effects of Fosters lager.

I look at him and grin.

"You still worried about Kirkie's mob?"

George shakes his head.

"Nah. Sod 'em. It's going to be a great night."

I finish my own can.

"Yeah," I say.

Dylan's finished preening. It's time to do one. Robbie switches the TV off and we all head for the door.

Outside, the day is finally cooling down. The sky is still the cloudless blue it's been all afternoon, but the sun is slowly sinking beyond the fields of caravans and chalets. The aroma of barbecues fills my nostrils. I get a tingle of excitement and anticipation. There's anxiety too, but it's good stuff, not bad. It's only a few minutes until I see Steph again. I don't know what might happen tonight. But I can't wait to find out.

There's a steady trickle of people wandering through Green Zone in the direction of the Family Entertainment Centre. We join the flow, then peel off to the left as we get into Blue Zone. A row of chalets stretches out in front of us.

"What number are we looking for?" Dylan asks.

"Blue 29," George says.

It seems to be even numbers on the right, odd numbers on the left, starting high and getting lower. We've gone past number 53, so it shouldn't be much further. Up in front I see four little kids kicking a football around and generally making a nuisance of themselves. It's our mates from Green Zone. They're a bit further from home today.

"How you doing, you lot?" I say.

The lad in the *Ben10* T-shirt looks us up and down.

"Still haven't pulled then," he says.

Dylan's eyes glint.

"Ha. That's where you're wrong. We're meeting some birds in a minute."

The girl in the pink cowboy boots pulls a face.

"Yeah, right," she says.

We keep walking. We're nearly there now, going down through the thirties. Gemma's chalet is the next on the left. It looks freshly painted. The plant tubs and the patch of lawn outside are neat and tidy. In the far corner there's a gnome in a Crystal Palace kit.

The girls have seen us coming. The door of the chalet swings open. It's Gemma. She looks nice. Hair pinned back, black vest and jeans.

"Hiya boys," she says, giggling.

It's not just us who've made a start on the night's drinking, it would seem.

"Alright?" George says. "You lot ready?"

"Yeah, we're about there."

Nikita's the next one out. She looks good too, in a blue sequinned top, shorts and a pair of gladiator sandals. There's only Steph still to come. And when she does, she looks stunning. Her hair is down tonight, a chin length bob, and she's in a short military-style khaki dress, black leggings and red Converse.

"You look great," I say. It's out of my mouth before I can stop myself.

Steph takes it in her stride.

"You too. That shirt's really nice against your skin now you've caught the sun."

I'm chuffed.

"Thanks."

We're almost ready to go. Gemma locks the chalet and puts the key in her shoulder bag. She sees me looking at the Crystal Palace gnome and raises her eyebrows.

"It's Granddad's," she says. "Don't ask."

We get off, following the traffic down to the court-yard. A big queue is forming outside the Family Entertainment Centre. I hope they haven't all arrived hoping to see Colin Wells. Over by Happy Valley, Vic Whitley is leaning against the wall, fag in hand. I'd recognise the red blazer and the grey trousers anywhere. Vic's got a busy night in front of him. He's probably going to have to pull a double shift on the bingo now.

There's nothing else for us to see. Whitbourne is beckoning. The night starts here.

We're about to go into the foyer when the kids appear again. They've been in the Wonderland Supermarket, buying sweets. I smile and give them a wave. They look at us. They look at the girls. They look at each other. Then they run off whooping and screaming. In a funny way I feel proud. We've shown them. They won't doubt us again.

Steph gives me a puzzled frown.

"It's a long story," I say.

eleven

It's a beautiful evening on Whitbourne seafront. As we pass the pine trees, a flock of starlings is coming in to roost. It's an amazing sight, like something you'd see on a nature programme. There's thousands of them. They're sweeping and curling in the sky like a swarm of bees. Little clusters are breaking off into separate black pulsing blobs, then rejoining the main swarm, until eventually the whole flock dives down and disappears into the branches, twittering and screeching.

A few people are still on the beach. The bloke with the big earphones and the metal detector who we saw yesterday, and a group of twenty or so Spanish kids sitting in a circle singing *Wonderwall* while one of them strums a guitar and another one plays the bongos. It's low tide. Two thirds of the pier is out of the water and the groynes are standing high and dry, covered in seaweed and barnacles.

As we get to the bandstand, the Whitbourne Concert Ensemble is in full swing. There's quite a good turn-out in the deckchairs and the musicians look smart in their dinner jackets. The conductor is working himself into a frenzy, waving his baton like he's dancing on hot coals. We stand and listen for a while.

"What are we going to do then?" I ask.

"We've got to go on the pier," Gemma says. "I always go with my granddad. You can't come to Whitbourne and not go on the pier."

"I'm definitely up for that," Nikita says.

We're all nodding.

It doesn't take us long to get to the pier. We hang a right off the seafront and walk under the archway. Music is playing from speakers overhead. Spandau Ballet. *True.* One of my mum's favourites.

I look left and right. At our gang. At Steph.

I've got a strange feeling. At this precise point in time, absolutely anything is possible. We've got the whole of our lives in front of us, and we just can't fail. Everything seems beautiful and perfect. I think it's because there's a kind of magic about piers. I've been on a few in my time, and I love them all. Blackpool, Brighton, Great Yarmouth. Whitbourne pier is half the size of those ones, and it's pretty scruffy. But it's still got that certain something.

We pass between a newsagent and a doughnut shop and keep going towards the amusement arcade, lured by the big red flashing neon letters spelling out *FUNTASTICA* above the entrance. Slatted benches run along both sides of us, and behind the benches there are white-painted iron railings, chipped and peeling, inset with a motif of two intertwined blue dolphins. Piles of red and white striped deckchairs are chained up, waiting for tomorrow. Up at the end of the pier, past Funtastica and the Waterfront Bar, a group of ten or eleven year old lads are chucking themselves off into the water and swimming like rats around the rusty stanchions holding the whole thing up.

We head into Funtastica. Flashing lights, beeping machines and toy grabbers are everywhere. The carpet is like a psychedelic nightmare. There's a casino area to the left, pool tables and air hockey to the right. Up in the arched roof there's a life-size model of a clown going round and round in circles with a propeller on his head and another one doing tricks on a trapeze.

"Whoa!" George says, obviously impressed.

He's not the only one. We're like a bunch of kids let loose in a toyshop. Even Robbie and Gemma, who've seen it all before. We set off across the arcade, looking for things to waste our money on, weaving through the punters, dodging the ferrety under-tens scuttling about checking the coin return slots.

There are two enormous girls on the dancing machine, so we stand and watch them, trying not to get caught laughing. One of them has got what looks like an arse hanging under the front of her pink puffa jacket, jiggling like a plate of white jelly. Presumably it's her stomach, but it's got a crack down the middle.

We've finished looking around now. Gemma and George have gone for the fruit machines, Robbie is settling down at a driving game and Dylan and Nikita are on *Whack-A-Mole*. That leaves me and Steph.

"What do you fancy then?" I ask.

Steph points to the far corner.

"Penny Falls."

"Nice one," I say. I like old-fashioned games.

I sift out two pounds and go to get some change.

The woman in the booth stops texting and looks up from her *Heat* magazine long enough to take my money and hand over a couple of bags of coins. I toss one to Steph and we make for the Penny Falls.

Ten minutes later we still haven't fed all the coppers into the machine. Every time we're nearly out there's a big cascade from one of the shelves and another heap of coins falls out. All the others have finished now and they're wanting to get off.

I look at Steph.

"You about done?"

Steph puts a last penny into the slot and watches it rattle its way down onto the top layer. Nothing drops. She nods.

I bag up all our coins and hand them to a little black lad who's been watching us. His dad sees what I've done and smiles.

I check my watch. Nearly nine.

"Where to now?" I ask.

"I think we should go for a drink," Gemma says. "We could try The Waterfront Bar."

We go out of the side doors and back onto the walkway. Lights are coming on all across Whitbourne. The streetlights along the seafront and the strings of fairy lights along the pier. We turn left and pass a hot dog kiosk, a café and some gift shops. The Waterfront Bar is up ahead.

Last night at Wonderland I was worried about us being asked how old we were. As we push through the doors into the Waterfront, I see it's not going to be a problem tonight. Compared to some of the kids in here, Dylan looks like a pensioner.

George and Gemma go to find some seats. The

rest of us head off to get the drinks.

The bloke behind the bar has overdone it with the piercings. He's got a nose ring, a stud under his bottom lip and what look like corks in his earlobes. There's a row of TVs along the wall to the right, all showing different things. Music videos. *Sky Sports*. One of those DVDs with an endless loop of spectacular car crashes. *They All Walked Away*, or something like that.

Robbie buys the round. Pints of Fosters for the lads, WKD for the girls. Dylan and Nikita stay by the bar while we pick up the glasses and bottles and go to join the others.

I take a seat and have a sip of my pint. As I put it back on the table, I notice something. George and Gemma are holding hands. I do a double-take. They're not making a big fuss of it or anything, but they're not hiding it either. I'm just getting my head round it all when I spot Dylan and Nikita outside one of the fire exits. They're not holding hands like George and Gemma. They're kissing.

Robbie's seen what's going on too. He leans over and whispers in my ear.

"Better get your act together, Chrissy Boy. You're being out-pulled by George and Dylan."

He's only pissing about, but he's got a point.

I look at Steph. She's gazing out of the windows at the sunset. Her fingers are curled around her bottle of WKD. She's got pink nail varnish on. I try to work out what she's thinking, but I'd never make a mind-reader.

Suddenly I feel really under pressure. Like I'm on trial. I don't want to let my chance with Steph pass me by, but I don't know what's the best thing to do. I've always been too shy to make the first move with girls. I wait for them to make a move on me. But what happens if Steph never does? Is she waiting for me? Or has the thought not even occurred to her? Questions, questions, questions.

Dylan and Nikita are coming towards our table now. Dylan sits down and Nikita stays standing up. She motions to Steph and Gemma and they all trot off to the toilets.

Across from me, George and Dylan are sitting there smirking.

"The girls have got a lot to talk about," Dylan says.

Robbie kicks my chair leg.

"Bet your ears are burning."

"Why's that then?" I ask.

"Because the girls will all be wondering what's up with you, you nob. What are you waiting for? A written invitation? Steph's yours. Seal the deal."

I rub my face with my hands.

"I dunno," I say. "I don't want to make a tit of myself."

Robbie rolls his eyes.

"But what's the worst that can happen?"

I shrug.

"I dunno," I say again. "I don't want to mess up. I really like her."

I'm expecting Robbie to laugh, but he doesn't. He just nods.

"I know you do, mate," he says.

I have a mouthful of beer and sigh.

On the other side of the table, Dylan and George

raise their glasses to one another. They knock them together, then George puts back half his pint in one go. He has a short break then he swigs down the rest.

I puff out my cheeks.

"You'll regret that later."

George belches. I don't think he's bothering with sensible drinking tonight.

The girls are coming back from the toilet. If they've been talking about me they're not letting on.

Steph sits next to me. As she smoothes out her dress, her hand brushes against mine. It might be a sign, but I can't be sure.

Over the next twenty minutes or so, we all take it easy. Drinking, talking, watching the TVs. I have a trip to the Gents, and on the way back I see there's some news about Letchford Town on *Sky Sports*. A possible takeover by a Saudi consortium with a five-year plan to make the club one of the giants of European football.

Dylan almost falls off his chair laughing.

"Yeah, right. Like that's going to happen. From League Two to the Nou Camp."

Robbie stretches.

"You never know."

"Wait until the Saudis get a look at the middle of Letchford," Dylan says. "If the Ainsdale Centre doesn't put them off, nothing will."

It goes quiet again. I sneak a look at Steph. She's still not giving out any signals. I'm starting to feel a bit of desperation. How come Dylan and George have cracked it and I haven't? That can't be right.

It's nearly half past nine. The concert at the bandstand is getting close to the big finale. I recognise the music from the 1812 Overture as it drifts across the beach.

"Come on," I say, draining my pint. "Let's go outside and watch the fireworks."

There's a murmur of agreement round the table. Everyone gets up.

We go out of the bar and turn left. Down on the beach the Spanish kids are still around, but the bloke with the metal detector is long gone. We pass a bait and tackle shop and a fortune-teller's booth and keep going until we get to the far end of the pier. The sea is churning against the framework of metal girders under our feet. We stand in a line along the railing, looking out across the water. The sun is sliding lower and lower into the sea, lighting up the whole sky with a reddish tinge, glinting off the roof of the bandstand.

Steph takes in the whole scene.

"It's beautiful," she says.

I'm about to say something when there's a crash of cymbals and a cluster of rockets are screaming into the dusk from the beach behind where the Whitbourne Concert Ensemble are playing, exploding in showers of red and green.

For the next two minutes the fireworks keep coming, one after the other. It's a brilliant display, just like Robbie said it would be. The 1812 Overture is reaching a crescendo, explosions are thudding and echoing and multi-coloured sparks are cascading like fountains over the water. Robbie's wandered across to film it all on his phone. Glancing to my left I see Dylan and Nikita kissing. George and Gemma are whispering to each other.

I look at Steph. My stomach is turning itself inside out. If I don't make my move I know I'll regret it for as long as I live. I've got to kiss her. And I've got to do it right now. I'm ninety-nine percent sure she feels the same way. But if I've misjudged it, if she looks at me like I've gone mad, that won't just be the weekend spoilt. I'll never recover. I might as well throw myself into the sea.

I draw a huge breath and instinct takes over. Leaning across, I grab Steph's hands and pull her towards me. And even as I'm doing it, I know it's going to be okay. As another rocket whizzes through the twilight, our lips meet and there's no holding back. I've kissed a few girls, but it's never been like this. Steph's mouth is soft and warm and moist and sweet. I close my eyes and it's like I'm flying.

One final rocket scorches into the sky, and then the concert is over. The fireworks are finished and the band has stopped playing. All that's left is a smell of gunpowder on the warm night air, and the faint sound of applause. When the clapping ends, everything is strangely calm and quiet.

I pull away from Steph. A couple of inches, so we're looking into each other's eyes. She smiles.

"That took you long enough," she says, giggling. "I thought I was going to have to jump on you."

I give her a grin.

"I like to play it cool," I say.

We both know I'm lying.

Robbie catches my eye. He winks, then he looks away.

We all stand and watch as the last rays of the sun

disappear. My arm is around Steph's waist and hers is around mine. I'm on top of the world. It's another amazing memory. A few more minutes and the sky finally goes dark. It's time to head back indoors.

It's busier in the Waterfront now. All the chairs and tables are taken. Nikita gets another round in and we stay standing at the bar, watching the TV screens, listening in on an ugly bloke chancing his arm with a girl who's obviously not interested. The bloke's a gawky type, in the kind of T-shirt George would wear on a bad day. *Free Hot Dog* in big red letters and an arrow pointing to his cock. He definitely thinks he's in with a shout, but he's getting nowhere. Eventually the girl turns her back and walks off.

Robbie cringes.

"Oh man, that was cold," he says.

The bloke in the *Free Hot Dog* T-shirt orders himself another pint. Right on cue, a car on *They All Walked Away* crashes and burns.

By quarter past ten we've all finished our drinks. I put the empties on the bar.

"What are we doing now then?" I ask. "Staying for another in here, or hitting the town?"

"I reckon town," Dylan says.

I turn to Robbie.

"Know any good pubs mate?"

Robbie shrugs.

"Nah. Pubs aren't my mum and dad's thing. We don't go into town at night."

I nod. It's not a problem. We'll work it out for ourselves.

We leave the bar and head in the direction of the

seafront. As we come past Funtastica, I glance through the door. The toy grabbers are calling to me.

"Wait a sec," I say. "I want to try something. It won't take long."

The arcade is as full as it was earlier, if not fuller. The lights are still blinking and flashing, faster than ever. Although it's getting late there are still lots of ferrety kids about, keeping an eye on the games players, waiting for money to drop into trays or under the machines. A big security guard in a red fleece with *Here To Help* on the back is monitoring the situation. The enormous girls are off the dancing game now. They've done their exercise for the night, and they're sitting over by the change booth digging into cones of chips and mayonnaise.

The grabber machines are lined up along the right-hand wall. There are lots of different toys to win. Teddies, The Simpsons, Looney Tunes. All kinds of stuff. I've got my eye on some South Park characters. I'm on a roll tonight.

While the others watch, I stick in a pound for four credits. Somewhere in the background, the chorus of *La Bamba* is repeating over and over. The green light comes on and I send the mechanical claw on its way. My first two efforts aren't up to much. With the third though, I manage to grab hold of Cartman and lift him straight up before he drops on top of Kenny. And with the fourth I hit the jackpot. Cartman comes tumbling down the chute.

I wheel round in triumph.

Steph squeals, throws her arms round my neck and gives me a kiss. Everyone starts clapping.

"Watch and learn," I say. "Watch. And. Learn."

I bend down and get Cartman out of the machine.
I hand him to Steph.

"Merry Christmas," I say.

twelve

As we return along the walkway, the moon is bathing the seafront in a silvery glow. It's a proper full moon tonight, bigger than I've ever seen it, a perfect disc hanging low in the pitch-black starry sky. It's lighting up the shabby old hotels so they look as white as fresh snow. It's like they've been mysteriously transported back in time, to the days when Whitbourne was on the up.

Soon we're at the entrance of the pier. It's not Spandau Ballet on the speakers any more. It's what they call easy-listening music. Something from another era. *Moon River*. It seems just right. Looking up, there's a sign across the archway. *Thank You For Visiting Whitbourne Pier. We Hope You Had A Good Time*. Yeah. I did, thanks.

I take Steph's hand and we lead the way across the road and up the street with the souvenir sellers and the rock shops. They're all closed up for the night. The shutters are down and the lights are off. The restaurants and cafes are still open though. The tables and chairs are still out on the pavements, but people are drinking now, not eating. We carry on past Poundtastic and come to a crossroads. I scan up and down the road, first right, then left. About fifty metres down there's a pub. The White Horse.

"What do you reckon?" I ask. "Shall we give it a go?"

Steph and Nikita are nodding.

"Worth a try," Dylan says.

It's dark inside the White Horse. The place reeks of stale beer, sweat and onions. Elvis is on the jukebox. The wall to the left is lined with benches, mostly occupied by old blokes. A black Labrador is lying on the floor. On the other side there's a raised area, surrounded by a waist-high barrier. Most of the seats are filled with younger people in their teens and twenties. Some of the wooden bars of the barrier are missing. I'm wondering what they might have been used for. A few of the customers look a bit dodgy.

Robbie taps me on the shoulder.

"We've made a blunder here."

"Yeah," I say. "You might be on to something."

There's some lads round a pool table over to the right. They're wearing hoodies and jeans. There's quite a bit of wet-look gel and cheap jewellery about. This is the style of boozer that Kirkie and his mates would hang around in.

"I think we should try somewhere else," Robbie says.

Nobody's arguing.

We go back outside and walk up the street, turning left and heading towards the main shopping area. We come past another rough-looking pub called Molly O'Shea's and a tattoo parlour and cut through the market place, trying not to gag on the smell of fish and rotting fruit. Someone's decapitated one of the pink plastic hippo bins and there's litter everywhere.

We're in the town centre now. No cars are about.

It's just taxis picking up and dropping off. Groups of blokes and groups of women are wandering around, looking for entertainment. Somewhere in the distance a seagull starts squawking in his sleep and about ten others join in.

"Anyone got any suggestions for which way we should go?" I ask.

There's blank looks all round. Roads and lanes are peeling off in every direction. Along an alley to the right, I think I can see a pub.

"Want to try down here?"

Everyone's in favour, so we set off.

The pub is called the Highcross Arms. Neatly trimmed trees are standing in buckets on either side of the entrance and in the doorway there's a gigantic bouncer in a white shirt and black tie. He's thirty stone at least. And it's muscle, not fat. If you turned him round, you could use his back as a cinema screen. He gives us a suspicious glance as we go past, but we don't look like we're going to cause any trouble.

I catch sight of our reflection in a mirrored wall. We were like a bunch of kids in Funtastica. We're not kids now. It might be the low lighting, but we look like we've all turned into adults in the last couple of hours. Scary. Life has started speeding up and we're getting carried along, ready or not.

I think about my mum and dad again. I wonder what they're doing while their sixteen year old son gets pissed at the seaside? Watching telly, I suppose. Or reading. I shouldn't be deceiving them like this. How many lies am I going to need to tell tomorrow evening? I feel a twinge of guilt. But then I remember something Steph said last night, talking about Nikita's parents. What they don't know isn't going to hurt them.

The Highcross Arms is the size of a barn. For some reason it smells like B&Q. My dad drags me round there on Sunday afternoons sometimes, when there's a crap match on *Sky*. As I take in the surroundings, the smell of paint and sawdust starts to make sense. The place looks like it only opened a couple of weeks ago. It's filled with shiny new furniture. The upholstery isn't covered in puke stains yet.

It seems to be a theme pub, but I'm not sure what the theme is. The walls are terracotta and there are Victorian-style lamps dotted about. On ledges, out of the reach of pissed idiots, there are aged-looking trinkets. Trombones and ships in bottles. To round it all off there's a fishing net suspended from the ceiling, filled with floats and shells and plastic puffer fish.

I squeeze Steph's hand.

"You lot get us somewhere to sit," I say, leaning close so she can hear me over the music that's blasting out. "We'll get the drinks in."

The girls set off and us lads head in the other direction.

It's crowded at the bar. While we're waiting, I try to suss the place out. Most of the people are quite young. Older than in the Waterfront, but not by much. Judging by the accents, it's a mix of locals, tourists and people down from London. The good thing is, everyone's dressed smartly. We're not going to bump into Kirkie in here.

A gap appears in front of me and I wriggle into it.

I'm up at the bar now, and the rest of the lads are behind me. I scan the beer pumps to see if they've got Fosters. They have. I put a twenty pound note between my fingers and try to attract someone's attention. Normally I'd let George take over but he's well away. I told him he'd regret knocking back that pint earlier. His eyes are in different orbits. It won't be long before he's wheeling out his *everyone likes a drink* patter.

A barman is heading my way. A flick of my twenty pound note and he makes eye contact.

"Four pints of Fosters please mate," I say, quick as a flash. "And three bottles of WKD."

When the barman has pulled the pints and opened the bottles, I hand over my twenty and get a couple of quid change. I pass two pints to Dylan and get the other two myself. Robbie grabs the WKD bottles. George has got nothing to carry but it's probably for the best. He's having trouble walking a straight line.

Easing out into the main part of the pub, we start looking for the girls. It doesn't take long. Steph's waving from the corner by the front windows. We cut across and plonk the drinks down. The girls have done a good job. They've got two tables, pulled together, with three stools on one side and an uphol-stered bench on the other.

Steph shifts along the bench and I sit next to her. She slides her hand onto my knee and we kiss. I can't actually understand what my problem was earlier on. Why it took me so long to go for it. Whatever. I got there in the end. I look at Cartman sitting on the table, his little blue and yellow bobble hat, his red jacket and his scowling face, and I can't help smiling.

I spend the best part of the next hour nursing my pint. George stumbles up to the bar to get himself another, but I tell him not to bother with one for me. It's like a role-reversal. Now I'm the one trying to be sensible, drinking slowly, pacing myself. I want to remember everything that happens tonight.

Me and Steph aren't saying much, but it doesn't matter. We're communicating in other ways. A touch. A glance. It all feels right. Natural. I'm happy just looking at her. Her mouth. The slight curve to her nose. The smoothness of her skin. The way she moves. There's no doubt about it. She's a babe.

Around half past eleven I head into the toilets. They're pretty impressive. Spotless and smelling of pine needles. The pub owners have had a bright idea to stop people vandalising the place. On the wall behind the urinals there's a board, with chalk laid on. As I take a piss, I look at the messages. Most of them seem to have been written by *JAY*. He's so pleased and excited by his name, he's scrawled it about twenty times. When I've done up my flies, I pick up a stick of chalk and put *IS A WANKER* under the biggest *JAY*.

As I'm leaving, my eyes are drawn to the condom machine over by the mirrors. Automatically, my hand goes to my pocket, checking for change. I don't mean to do it. It just happens. I'm as bad as Dylan. But like Dylan, I shake my head and keep going. The thing is, however much I'd like to break my duck, if I ended up in bed with Steph tonight, it wouldn't be right. She deserves better than that. It'll happen, but it might be months away. I know we live miles apart, but we're going to keep on seeing each other. I just know it.

Back in the pub things are starting to get confusing. I've been doing my best to fend it off, but pissedness is creeping up on me. My face is warm and I'm starting to feel slightly disconnected from reality. I'm still stringing sentences together, but it's taking a lot of concentration.

Midnight is on the way and I keep losing track of people. I think the girls are in the toilets. Robbie's off talking to a fit-looking blonde bird who's been giving him the eye. I don't know where George is. Me and Dylan are the only ones left here at the table.

Sometimes Dylan's a bit difficult to talk to. Certainly harder than Robbie, who I've always had loads in common with. But it shouldn't be hard to find common ground with Dylan tonight. We've both had a result. I swill the dregs of my pint round the glass then knock them back.

"Hey, Dylan," I say, putting the glass down. "We've scored. We've genuinely scored. Steph's amazing and Nikita's well nice, you jammy bastard."

"Yeah," Dylan says.

I'd thought he'd be as chuffed as I am. But even in my numb state I can see he isn't. He drums his fingers on the table and sighs.

"What's up?" I ask, puzzled.

Dylan frowns.

"I was thinking about after the summer."

"What about it?"

Dylan's struggling to say what he wants to say. He has another go.

"Well, you and Robbie and George are going back to college and I'm going to be working for Cawsey Contractors."

I nod. I don't know where he's going with this.

"Well," he says again, "you lot are still going to be together. Maybe, you know, you won't be wanting to hang around with me any more."

I get it now. I can't think of anything to say. I'm amazed. I'd never have guessed he might be thinking like that. This is Dylan. Mr Macho. The hardest man on Earth. But he's changed a lot this weekend. We all have. Well, me, Dylan and George for definite. Maybe not Robbie so much. But perhaps he doesn't need to change. As I look over, I see he and the blonde girl are taking pictures of each other with their mobiles. The boy leads a charmed life.

Dylan wipes his hand across his face. He swallows.

"It just guts me to think I might lose contact with you all."

I'm getting over the shock now. I reach out and put my hand on Dylan's arm. He's not the touchy-feely type, but he doesn't flinch.

"Don't be stupid mate," I say. "We'll never lose contact."

Dylan looks at me.

"Honest?"

"Honest. And anyway, we're going to want to bum money off you when you're earning. You'll never get rid of us."

Dylan laughs. He looks more like his old self.

"Thanks Chris," he says.

I shrug.

"No problem."

Dylan tugs at my elbow.

"And you won't say anything about this, will you?"

I mime zipping my lips shut.

The girls have reappeared. Steph gives me a peck on the cheek as she sits down. Dylan's forgotten all his worries and he starts stroking Nikita's hair. Everyone's happy except for Gemma. She's craning about in her chair, looking concerned. She puts her hand on my arm.

"Where's George?" she asks.

"Dunno," I say.

This information takes some time to sink in. Gemma's wrecked. I notice she's been reapplying her lipstick. There are bits of red smudged on her teeth.

"I want to know where my Georgie is," she says.

Steph takes a slug of WKD.

"Any chance of you having a look for him?" she asks. There's an apologetic tone to her voice. "Gemma's a bit of a worrier."

"Yeah," I say. "No problem."

I have to admit I'm a bit worried about George myself. He might have got lost. I've never seen him as pissed as he's been this weekend. Last night, he was well out of it. Tonight he's absolutely steaming.

I go into the crowd, keeping my eyes peeled. In general it's not too difficult to spot George, but there's no sign of him now. I'm standing still for a moment when someone pinches my arse. I turn round. Robbie.

I shake my head.

"Oh. You're back are you? Thought you'd be with that bird for the rest of the night."

Robbie shrugs.

"Nah. She's here with her mum and dad. She had to go back to their B&B. They've got this landlady who stands at the door in a hairnet and locks up if they're not in by one. I've got her number though. She lives not far from us. Sleaford. We're going to get together when we're back."

I laugh. Like I said. A charmed life.

"Anyway," I say. "Have you seen George? He's gone AWOL."

Robbie strokes his chin.

"Bet I know where he is," he says.

I've got a good idea too.

Inside the toilets, five blokes are standing at the urinals. None of them is George. There are four cubicles along the far wall. We cut across and start trying the doors. The first two are empty, but the third and fourth are locked.

I knock at the nearest one.

"Anyone in there?" I ask.

"Piss off," someone shouts. It's not George.

Robbie tries the last door.

"George?" he says.

There's a moan and the sound of a bolt being drawn back. The door swings inwards and we get our first glimpse of George. He's on all fours, spread-eagled over the bowl, getting reacquainted with his Chinese takeaway. There are beansprouts everywhere.

"Oh God," he says. "I feel like shit. I must have

had a bad pint."

I laugh.

"A bad four or five pints, more like."

George moans again.

"Come on," I say. "We'd better get you sorted out. Gemma's fretting."

Robbie grabs one of George's arms, I get the other and we heave him round until he's sitting on the edge of the plastic seat. I check him out for signs of puke. It looks like he's okay. I have a glance over his shoulder at the contents of the bowl. My stomach churns. The toilet has got one of those motion-activated flushes. I pass my hand in front of the sensor and send his dinner on its way.

George stares down at the floor. He looks like he's about to cry.

"Everyone likes a drink," he says in his broadest Brummie twang. "But no-one likes a drunk."

Robbie fishes in his pocket and comes out with a packet of Polos.

"Here you are. Have one of these. Your breath's going to stink."

George takes a mint and gives the packet back. He runs his hands through his hair and pats it flat again.

I get a handful of bog roll, wet it under the cold tap and bring it back for George to dab his face with. Make himself look a bit more presentable. Not that Gemma's going to be paying any attention. She's as pissed as he is.

By the time we're out of the toilets it's nearly quarter to one. The pub has started emptying as people head home or go on to nightclubs. Back in our corner, Dylan and Nikita are all over one another and Gemma's fast asleep. I help Robbie manoeuvre George onto the bench beside Gemma and I sit down next to Steph. She looks extra pleased to see us. She's not had anyone to talk to for a while.

"We should get going," I say. "Some people are struggling."

Steph smiles at George and Gemma. She knows who I mean.

I look at Robbie. He agrees.

I check the bottles and glasses on the table. Everyone's drinks are gone. I nudge Dylan.

"We're going to get off."

Dylan nods and whispers something in Nikita's ear that makes her giggle.

George shakes Gemma awake and they lever themselves up against the back of the bench. Steph gets Cartman. Finally we're all ready.

"Okay," I say. "Let's make a move."

thirteen

"Shit," Dylan says as we step into the street. "What's happened?"

I look around. Whitbourne has changed while we've been in the Highcross Arms. Everywhere I turn, it's carnage. Blokes pissing in shop doorways, drunks lying in the gutters, people bleeding, women crying.

"This is why my mum and dad don't come here at night," Robbie says.

We start up the alley towards the centre of town, doing our best to avoid the casualties. I'm up front with Steph. Dylan and Nikita are behind us. Robbie's at the back end, shepherding Gemma and George along.

Being out in the fresh air seems to be having an effect on me. And not a good one. The pissedness that was creeping up in the pub has taken complete hold now. It's all getting a bit surreal. The sounds of Whitbourne at night are muffled and other-worldly. All around me, shop windows are filled with bright coloured lights. I feel as if I'm floating along in an insulated technicolour bubble.

Steph glances back in time to see George staggering off the edge of the kerb. His legs are like elastic bands. Gemma tries to help him stay upright and ends up touching down herself.

Steph pulls a face. She seems completely sober.

"I think we should try to find something to eat," she says. "Something to soak up all the booze those two have put away."

"Mmm," I say. I leave it at that. I'm a bit worried I might be slurring my words. In the pub, with the loud music, it wasn't so obvious. Out here, there would be no hiding it. I don't want Steph to think I'm a lightweight.

I spot a chippy on the corner. There's a queue, but it's not too long. We peer through the window. A big doner is twirling on a spit at the back, while a hairy bloke in a vest shaves bits off it with a knife. There's a lovely smell in the air, but maybe a doner and chips isn't the best meal for Gemma and George at this point in time. We keep going.

Up in the main shopping area there's more carnage. Two women are having a screaming match that's just on the verge of turning physical. There's a bloke face down in a wooden tub of petunias. Another one is sitting on the plinth of a statue. His shirt is hanging off him in strips.

We still need to find somewhere to eat. Over on the far side of the square I see a familiar sight. Down a narrow lane, the big yellow *M* of McDonald's.

Steph's seen it too. We look at each other and nod.

Maccy D's is warm and bright and packed. Gentle music is playing, keeping everyone calm. People are milling around aimlessly, with and without trays, and the food queues are stretching back to the door. I figure we're going to be eating out in the street until a group of girls stands up and moves away from a table down to the left. Dylan and Nikita are off like a shot, gathering as many chairs as they can while Robbie steers George and Gemma through the crowd.

Me and Steph stay standing up.

"We'll get the food," I say, pleased to hear that my voice sounds okay after all. "Big Mac meals, yeah?"

"Spot-on," Robbie says.

Steph tosses Cartman across to Nikita, then we join the end of a queue. There are a lot of staff working and it's not long until we're getting near the counter. A bearded bloke in a lilac shirt is standing at the bottom of the food chutes keeping his minions on their toes. He's barking orders into the cooking area like Whitbourne's own Gordon Ramsay.

The girl at the till gives me an unconvincing smile. According to her name badge, she's called Cleo.

"Seven Big Mac meals, please," I say.

Cleo frowns.

I feel like I need to explain.

"They're not all for me."

Cleo grunts and taps the screen in front of her.

"What drinks would you like with those?" she asks.

I look at Steph.

"Diet Cokes?"

I nod, turning back to Cleo.

"Yeah. Diet Cokes with all of them, please."

Cleo punches the information into her till. I settle the bill and Cleo sets about piling two trays with seven Big Mac meals. Steph gets the food, I get the drinks and we weave across to where the rest of the gang are sitting, stopping off to get straws, serviettes and mini paper cups of sauce on the way.

Back at the table we unload the trays. I open my Big Mac box, tip my fries into the lid and take a huge gulp of my Diet Coke. It's nice to have something other than lager pouring down my throat.

George and Gemma are still looking rough, propped against each other like two fallen trees after a gale. Robbie and Dylan are starting to show the effects of a second evening of boozing. The only people who are still full of life are Steph and Nikita. I'm somewhere in between, trying hard to keep myself on the straight and narrow.

I look around the restaurant for something to concentrate on. The floor is polished grey tiles. The tables are matt green formica and the seats are padded with fake brown leather. To the left is a flight of stairs leading to a first floor. There are posters on the walls of Happy Meal toys and giant-size Quarter Pounders With Cheese and McChicken Sandwiches. In my muddled state, none of it seems to mean anything.

I lift the top off my burger, fish out the gherkins and dump them in my empty fries carton. I take a bite of my Big Mac. As I chew, my eyes settle on the piece of paper lining one of the trays. Facts and figures about the benefits of taking an hour of exercise every day. It's the sort of stuff I wouldn't normally bother with, but right now it's just the thing to focus my mind. Slowly but surely, the bubble I've been floating in starts to melt away.

The restaurant gradually gets less busy over the next half an hour. There's nobody wanting our table, so we take our time, letting the food go down.

Dylan squashes his Big Mac box and shoves it into his empty drink cup.

"What are we going to do next then?" he asks. "It's only just gone one o'clock."

Robbie rummages with his finger in his ear.

"We could hit the clubs," he says.

I point at George and Gemma.

"Do you think they'd let those two in?"

Nobody needs to answer that. George looks at me. He knows I'm talking about him, but he doesn't know what I'm saying. He grins a dazed grin.

"Stop messing," he says.

Nikita's got a suggestion.

"We should finish up in here, then get a couple of taxis back to Wonderland. We can carry things on back there, either in the chalet or in your caravan."

That sounds like a good call. I smile and nod, looking at Steph. She smiles too.

We all start piling our rubbish onto the trays, getting ready to go. As I stand up, I hear a noise from the first floor. A bit of rowdiness. There's a group of lads coming down the stairs. Six of them, led by a big bloke with gelled hair and dodgy Nikes.

Without a word, I dive into my seat again.

Steph's seen who it is. She almost crushes my hand in hers.

"Keep low," she hisses.

Robbie and Dylan have got their backs to the staircase, but they can see that something's up.

"Kirkie," I whisper.

The lads are at the bottom of the steps now. They're shouting and swearing, hanging off one another. The one who looks like a bulldog in a woolly hat pulls a handful of straws from the dispenser and throws them onto the floor. He looks around at his mates, a hurt expression crossing his face as he realises none of them has noticed. There's some more shouting, a few threats aimed at staff and customers, and they're making for the exit.

I let out a breath and collapse against the back of my chair. Kirkie's in the street and his mates are following. As long as we keep our heads down for the next minute or so, it'll all be okay.

The last of the gang through the door is the little kid in the red cap. Just before he leaves he turns, sweeping his eyes across the whole restaurant. As a reflex, I put my hand up to cover my face. I don't think he's seen me. But I know who he *has* seen. The bloke it's almost impossible to hide. George.

Red Cap's eyes light up. He grabs the collar of the lad in front of him and shouts into the street for Kirkie and the rest to come back.

The world seems to have slowed to half speed. I don't know if that's good or bad. It's giving me time to think, but the thoughts aren't nice. I find myself scanning back over the entire history of our problems with Kirkie's lot. How it's escalated. What would have happened if we'd got to that pedestrian crossing a couple of seconds earlier or later? What if Dylan hadn't grabbed his balls? I thought the whole thing was funny at first. It was even a bit of a joke on the beach. I'm not laughing now.

Kirkie's gang have all piled inside. As they advance, a horrible feeling of inevitability is sinking in. Third time unlucky. We're not going to be able to negotiate our way out of this one. There's not going to be policemen or lifeguards to break it up, and the local lads aren't looking to tax us now. They want our blood.

Nobody's saying anything. We're way beyond words. The other people in the restaurant are starting to take cover. They know this is serious shit. Kirkie's grinning. Lightbulb Head and Red Cap have got a kind of wild look on their faces. The other lads seem a bit less gung-ho, but the thing is, they're all ready to rumble. It's what they do. Not like us. I've never had a fight in my life and neither has Robbie. Dylan thinks he's hard but has never had to back it up, and George couldn't punch his way out of a wet paper bag.

I stand up and move round to the front of the table, keeping the girls out of the firing line. Robbie and Dylan follow suit. Even George is on his feet. Whatever happens next, we're as ready as we'll ever be. Gemma and Nikita are frozen where they sit. Steph's wearing the strange expression of fear mixed with sadness that I first saw last night. I still can't actually believe that it's all about to go off. It just doesn't compute. But then the lad in the white anorak with the red tartan shoulders is lunging across the table at me and I know it's for real. I swing my fist and hit something. His head? His elbow? I'm not sure. He totters backwards then lunges in again.

All hell is breaking loose. It's like one of those scenes in a martial arts film where the characters hover above the ground, executing somersaults and chops. But in here it's not black-clad Ninjas swishing about. It's chavs in caps and hoodies and baggy jeans and lime green Adidas. And instead of nunchucks and throwing stars and samurai swords, it's trays and half-filled cups of Diet Coke and melting ice cubes. There's not a lot of skill on show. If this was a martial arts film, the audience would be demanding their money back.

The whole restaurant is in chaos. The customers who haven't found cover yet are scattering all over the place, running and diving under tables, screaming and shouting. Outside the windows, concerned faces are peeping in wondering what all the noise is about. Behind the counter the staff are playing statues, mouths open, eyes wide. I notice the bloke in the lilac shirt, Gordon Ramsay, push a girl out of the way and scuttle off into the kitchen.

Considering we're outnumbered six to four and one of our gang is so pissed he can hardly stand up, we're not doing too badly in the first few seconds of combat. I manage to get hold of the tartan shoulders of the lad in the anorak as he has another go. I push him down onto the floor, aiming and missing with a couple of kicks. Robbie whacks the fat kid with the buck teeth in the mouth, sending the fag behind his ear skittering to the floor and Dylan launches a left hook at Bulldog Boy.

But that's only the first wave. The heavy artillery is up next. Lightbulb Head is coming for me, Kirkie's making for Robbie and Red Cap is arrowing in at George.

I duck down, but something crashes into the top of my skull, sending me sprawling across the table. Before I can get myself back upright there are punches whistling in from all directions. It's not just Lightbulb Head, it's the buck toothed kid too. I wrestle myself round and see that Kirkie's got Robbie in a headlock while Bulldog Boy swings his cheap trainers at Dylan. There's a ringing in my ears. I feel dizzy and sick. We're going to get battered.

George still doesn't know what's occurring. Red Cap is staring at him, goading him, while George stands there, arms dangling by his sides. Red Cap darts to the left then jumps forward. Without thinking, George clenches his fist and brings it up to defend himself. And as he does, he connects flush with Red Cap's jaw. There's a crunching sound and Red Cap spins round, crashing to the floor. It looks like he's out cold.

The fighting stops. There are confused looks all round. This wasn't supposed to happen. Red Cap is moving now, pushing himself up. And as he gets to his feet, Gemma starts screaming.

At first I don't know what's going on. But then I see. A flash of silver in Red Cap's hand. He's got a blade. He's been made to look like a twat and now he wants payback. His little eyes are glittering with hatred.

Gemma lets out another high-pitched, eardrum-shattering scream. The sound is so loud, so startling, that everyone seems to be rooted to the spot. Even Kirkie and his boys. In that split second a channel opens up, right through the middle of the restaurant, all the way to the door. It's our chance to run and we've got to take it. This isn't the time or place to be playing the hero. Somebody's going to be heading for the mortuary.

"Go," I yell. "Go."

Snatching up a chair and making like a lion-tamer, I stand guard as Steph leads the charge to the street. Once everyone's past me, I chuck the chair and leg it.

Once we're outside, I grab Steph's hand, check everyone's with us, put my head down and run. We race back up the alley heading for the middle of town, dodging through the nightclubbers and the pissheads. I spin round, hoping to see that we're in the clear, that Kirkie's mob haven't bothered to give chase, but it's bad news. They're bundling out of the doors and charging after us like a pack of wild dogs, skittling people all over the place.

In the central shopping area we bear left towards a T-junction then go right at Primark, in the general direction of the Bus Depot. We're flying along on pure adrenaline, but in the corner of my eye I can see George is running out of steam. His head is starting to droop and his arms and legs aren't flailing the way they were a few hundred metres back. He stumbles across the pavement, grabs hold of a lamppost and hangs on like a drowning man. He's fighting for air, wheezing like a pair of bellows.

We all skid to a halt. Gemma's on the point of crying, but there isn't time for sympathy. I take hold of the front of George's shirt and try to yank him along with me. It's no good. He won't let go of the lamppost. I shoot a glance back down the street. We've put quite a bit of distance between us and the locals, but this is giving them the chance to close the gap. I finally manage to pull George away from the post, manhandling him round to face me.

157

"George, you're going to get us killed," I scream. I mean it. I'm shaking him like a huge rag doll, trying to get the message across.

George's eyes are vacant. I look over his shoulder and see Lightbulb Head, Red Cap and Bulldog Boy steaming our way. I shake him again and he snaps back to the real world. He blinks a couple of times and nods to show that he knows what's needed.

We set off again, hurtling hard and fast, along past the crossing where all our troubles started. The further out of town we get, the darker it is. Only one in five streetlights seems to be working. My lungs are burning and everything around me is a blur. Without warning, a drunken bloke in a red fez staggers out from behind a wheelie bin, shouting and shaking drips from his dick. Robbie, Dylan and Nikita skip round him and keep going, but I haven't got time to adjust my stride. The next thing I know, I'm flat on the tarmac, staring up at the night sky framed by the faces of Steph, Gemma and George.

Steph's the one close to tears now.

"Chris," she says, her voice cracking. "Chris, you've got to get up."

I don't know if I'm hurt or not, but my adrenaline's still in full flow. I scramble up, looking back along the road, expecting to see Kirkie's mob charging into view, but there's no sign of them. A thought crosses my mind. We might have got away. The bloke in the fez is groaning, pulling himself onto all fours.

"You alright?" Steph asks, calmer now.

I shake out my arms and legs, checking that they're working. They seem to be. There's grit embedded in

158

my hands, my knees are skinned and my head's throbbing, but apart from that I'm in one piece.

"Yeah, reckon so," I say. "You'd better check on him, though." I point to the spot where Fez Man was grovelling a few seconds before, but he's already on his feet, shuffling his way back to the sights and sounds of Whitbourne town centre.

Robbie and the others have twigged what's happened now, and they're jogging back to where we're standing.

"I think we've lost them," I say, picking a stone out of my right palm.

Dylan nods.

My grazed knees are stinging. I pull up my left trouser leg to inspect the damage. It's not nice, but so what? We've given Kirkie and Co the slip. I look back along the road again. If the local lads were still on the hunt we'd definitely be able to see them. I roll my trouser leg down and straighten up. I feel great.

It doesn't last. Two hundred metres down, by the Health Centre, the headlights of two cars burst into life and the sound of revving engines and thudding music fills the air. It's the Citroen Saxo and the Peugot 205 we saw the lads in when we first arrived in Whitbourne. We haven't got away at all.

And we're in big, big trouble.

fourteen

The two cars lurch into gear and start closing in. A jolt of panic goes right through me. It's like being wired up to the mains. We turn and run. It's a primeval drive for survival keeping us going now. After hitting the deck, my equilibrium's shot to pieces. I'm losing track, but it looks like all our gang are still here. Now that Kirkie's lot have got wheels though, we're sitting targets. We've got to get off the main road.

I grip Steph's hand and drag her down a side street just as the cars screech past, missing the turning. It's bought us some time, but not much. We race down the middle of the road and go left, down a street of terraced houses, each one with a low front wall and brick gateposts. There's nowhere to hide. I'm already imagining the feeling of cold steel sliding between my ribs. We need a miracle. Fifty metres up, there might be one. In amongst all the cars squeezed in nose-to-tail, there's one that stands out. A dark, 3 Series BMW saloon.

"Steph," I shout, pointing. "Bimmer."

Steph's seen the motor and she knows exactly what I mean. There's no need to explain.

"Going to have to smash the window," she says. "Not got time to wedge the door."

My eyes start flicking around, searching for something to put through the tough glass. As we pull level with the car, I see what I'm after. A pair of concrete eagles, sitting on the gateposts of a stone-clad house. I get hold of the nearest one and yank it upwards. There's a crunching sound and the bird comes away, heavy in my hands, a big metal spike sticking out of the underside. In one movement I swing it through the air and crash it into the driver's side window of the BMW.

The sound of the alarm tears through the night. All up and down the street, lights are coming on and curtains are twitching but there's no time to worry about that. I lob the concrete eagle onto the path then stand back as Steph pushes her hand inside the car, springing the central locking system. Gemma dives into the front passenger side, Steph jumps into the driver's seat and the rest of us pile into the back, squashed in like sardines. I don't know who I'm on top of, I don't know who's on top of me.

As the doors are slammed shut, I squint between the front seats. Steph's scrabbling under the steering column, pulling away some clips and ripping down the plastic covering. A few more seconds, some twisting of wires, and the alarm cuts out. A few seconds after that, the engine roars into life. Steph guns the accelerator and we scream away from the kerb.

I'm going into a sort of sensory overload. Nothing seems logical or real any more. My brain can't process all the information. The growl of the engine. The squeal of tyres. The crunch of gears. The thudding of my heart, the rasping of my breath. The smell of perfume and aftershave and sweat and beer. The texture of upholstery as my face is pushed into it. The weight of people on top of me. Elbows and knees pressing into my ribs and thighs. The buildings and the lights flashing by. The force of being hurled from side to side as the big car swerves round corners. A hundred different emotions all at once.

Through it all, I'm starting to think we've escaped. It's the second time I've thought that. And for the second time, I'm wrong. Suddenly the car is filled with dazzling white light. It's the spots on the front of a pair of motors directly behind us. Kirkie's Saxo and the Peugot 205.

I lever myself up and catch fragments of what's going on. A freeze-frame image of Kirkie and Red Cap's snarling faces, leering through the windscreen of the Saxo. Steph swings right, then left. Down past CarpetWorld, up a terraced street, round a corner by a big church with thousands of flints set into its walls, round another corner, along a row of lockup garages.

The streets are like a maze, but Steph seems to have a sixth sense guiding her through. When she said she was quite a good driver, she wasn't telling the whole truth. She's unbelievable. We should be stuck down a cul-de-sac, being surrounded and getting the crap kicked out of us, or worse. But we're not. And something's changed. Our car isn't lit up now. It only seems like seconds since they were right on our tail, but we've lost Kirkie and his posse. We flash past Poundtastic and tear down the road with the souvenir shops and the cafes. The pier is coming up and we're away and free.

We could stop now, but we don't. There's still a chance Kirkie hasn't given up the chase. Turning right, we head out along the deserted seafront, past the bandstand, the lifeboat station and the pine trees. Soon we're beyond the last of the hotels, speeding out of town, following the road as it peels away from the coast and climbs into the hills. The entrance to Wonderland is a few hundred metres ahead. Steph moves down through the gears, swivelling round in her seat.

"Shall we ditch it here or keep going?" she asks. It's the first thing anyone's said since we got into the car.

A voice comes out of the pile of bodies on top of me. It's Robbie.

"Keep going. Head for Bellevue Point."

Steph nods and slides back up into fifth.

Beyond Wonderland, there are no streetlights any more. The back roads are steep and narrow and winding, hemmed in on both sides by overhanging trees. We come to a crossroads and Steph guides the car left, out across the downs and towards where England comes to an abrupt end. There's a sign just beyond the turning. *Bellevue Point 1 Mile.*

The road is still climbing, but the slope is much gentler now, flattening out as we get nearer to the cliffs. It's a strange, spooky landscape, illuminated by a moon that seems to have got even bigger as the night has gone on. The trees are further away, bent into hunched black silhouettes by a lifetime of pummelling by the wind off the sea. We've not seen another vehicle since we left Whitbourne. We're right out in the middle of nowhere, but there are signs of civilisation up ahead. The visitors' centre and the pub, shut down and silent.

Further on, the road arcs round to the right, running parallel to the cliff face, separated from the chalk precipice by a couple of hundred metres of downland. Moving through the gears again, Steph finds a place where the kerb isn't too high. She bumps the car across the pavement, onto the grass and up to the brow of the hill, finally stopping about twenty foot before the land drops away.

The engine cuts out and everything goes silent. The silence stretches on for what seems like ages. And then the laughing starts. It's wild, out-of-control laughing that keeps going and going, as we bundle out of the doors and roll onto the cool ground.

And we're not only laughing any more. We're screaming and yelling and whooping. We're buzzing. I don't know what might have happened back in Whitbourne if Kirkie's gang had got hold of us. But it feels like we've cheated death.

I push myself up and take Steph's hand. We walk to the cliff edge. When we're close, we lie on our stomachs. The grass is short and bristly, flat as a putting green, dotted with tiny plants. We inch forward, commando-style, until we're looking down into the void.

It's an awesome sight. The moon is shining like an immense torch, shimmering across the surface of the sea. Thousands of pinpricks of light are dancing off the waves and bouncing against the perfect white of the chalkface as it extends to the beach below. We're at the absolute top point of the whole ridge. A hundred and twenty-five metres above sea level, I remember Robbie said. Down near the bottom there's the remains of what looks like a flight of chalk steps leading up the cliff, coming to a sudden halt where years of wind and rain have washed them away. Over to the left, Whitbourne is a glittering grid of tiny lights. The pier is just visible as the bay curves round. A gentle breeze ruffles my hair. I find a stone to throw and watch it disappear into nothingness.

I look at Steph. She rolls her eyes. No words needed.

We both look back down to the beach. It's not sandy, and it doesn't have shingle like the stretch of coast near the bandstand. It's white chalk, smoothed by the pounding of the sea, pitted with potholes and strewn with green seaweed, like streamers from a big party long since finished. In the far distance I can see the lights of a ferry cutting across the sea on its way to France.

I clear my throat.

"Steph," I say, trying to put my thoughts in order. "Back there in town, you know, you...you probably saved someone's life."

Steph gives me an awkward smile. She tucks her hair behind her ear.

"Maybe. But we've got problems haven't we? I've twocced another motor, and our fingerprints are going to be all over it."

I nod. She's right. It's a problem. But to every problem there's a solution. And the solution is lying a hundred and twenty-five metres down the cliff. I don't know much about forensics, but I reckon if the

165

car was in the sea for a couple of days any fingerprints would be well and truly washed out of
existence.

Steph's read my mind. We both stand and run
back across to where the others are still lying.
There's no time to hang around.

"Come on," I shout. "We've got to dump the car."

While people are standing up and getting themselves ready, Steph pulls open the door of the BMW.
She leans across the driver's seat and releases the
handbrake. She slams the door again then runs
round to the back to join the rest of us and we begin
to push the big vehicle towards the cliff edge.

It's slow going at first, but as the last stretch of
grassy clifftop slopes downwards, the car starts to
pick up speed. The front wheels roll out into thin air
and the BMW stops with a jolt. Its underside
scrapes slowly forwards, pulled by the weight of the
engine, and the back wheels lift up. For a second I
think it's going to stay like that, balanced like a
huge seesaw, but then it steadily pitches forward
until the rear end is pointing skywards. It stays
there for a brief instant, then plunges out of sight.

Running to the edge of the cliff, we watch the
BMW hit a ledge and spiral wildly to the beach. A
sound like distant thunder rises up. I can actually
feel the rumbling in my body. There's no explosion,
and the car looks intact. It's even the right way up,
like someone's parked it there, a few metres from
the giant wall of chalk. We stand for a while, mes-
merised, then we walk back and flop onto the grass.

My body is coming down off red alert. My knees
hurt and my hands hurt. There's a lump on the top

of my head where I got punched in McDonald's and another one on the side from where I hit the tarmac. But it's no big deal. We're alive. That's what matters. We're all alive.

Steph touches my arm.

"I've got an admission to make," she says.

I tilt my head on one side.

"What's that?"

Steph sighs.

"I've lost Cartman."

I laugh.

"No worries. I'll win you another one tomorrow."

I lie back and stare up at the stars. Relaxation is spreading through me.

There's movement to my left. Gemma's standing up.

"Where's George?" she asks.

I'm not really paying attention.

"Where's George?" Gemma asks again, more urgently this time.

Nobody's answering her. I sit up. I scan from left to right. Steph's here. Nikita's here and Gemma's here. Robbie's here and so is Dylan. But there's no George. I feel the first little flicker of unease in the pit of my stomach.

I get up and look around. Perhaps George has gone off to take a piss behind one of the gnarled bushes down by the road.

But there's no sign of him.

The flicker in my guts is growing now. Like the fire last night, it's gradually catching light and the flames of unease are rising, moving from my stomach and working their way up my throat to the back of my mouth.

George isn't here.

I try to keep my tone steady, unemotional.

"Has anyone seen him? I mean, since we've been up here, has anyone seen George?"

There's no response.

My whole body feels like it's ablaze now. A terrible certainty is dawning on me. I know where George is. Five of us would never have got in the back seat of the BMW. So George would have made his own arrangements. He'd have done what he did last Friday, when we went into Letchford in Dylan's brothers' Escort. Squashed himself into a ball in the boot. And no-one's seen him since we got to the cliffs. So he's still in the boot.

This just can't be happening. I stand up and walk to the cliff edge, looking for the place where the BMW disappeared. The fresh scars on the grass help me find the exact point. Peering over into emptiness, I'm getting a strange feeling that the car might not be there. That this whole thing is a dream. And that in a minute I'm going to wake up in a puddle of my own piss and puke. It gives me a moment of hope. But I'm not dreaming. I can see the car. Water is starting to creep over the smooth chalk of the beach and lap gently around it.

I turn away. No-one needs to ask me what I'm thinking. We've all come to the same conclusion. The colour has drained from everyone's faces. In the pale light of the moon, we look like ghosts.

Gemma's still on her feet. She takes a couple of steps, sags down and starts to sob quietly. Steph and Nikita are rigid with shock. Robbie and Dylan have got their heads in their hands.

I walk across to where everyone's sitting and sink to my knees. Again, the same thought. This just can't be happening.

Dylan lifts his eyes to look out to the horizon.

"Instant Karma," he says. "That's what this is. Like George said. We all lied to our parents, and look what the result is. It's Instant Karma."

I shake my head. I can't let myself believe that. This weekend was supposed to be a laugh. A harmless laugh and a piss-up. We earned it. I know it's bad we did it behind our parents' backs, but it's not the crime of the century. We're not bad lads. George definitely isn't a bad lad. So why are we getting punished like this?

Gemma's sobbing is getting louder. Steph goes across to try to comfort her.

Dylan's eyes are still focused on the horizon.

"George didn't even want to leave Wonderland tonight. He said there would be trouble. The Family Entertainment Centre might have been shit, but if we'd stayed there then at least, you know..." his words trail away.

"Yeah," Robbie says. "And we bullied him. Ganged up on him. This is our fault. Not just that we pushed the car off. It's all our fault."

I shake my head again. It's true, but I don't want to think about it. The thing is, it's impossible not to. People are always using words like *disaster* and *tragedy* to describe crappy, everyday stuff. Like Letchford Town getting relegated. But this really is a disaster. This really is a tragedy. We've just killed our mate.

I get my phone out of my pocket and slide it open. It's ten to two. I select *MENU* and open my file of photos, flicking through until I get to the one George BlueToothed to me in the Wonderland Supermarket. The one taken by the bloke in the orange reflective jacket at Whitbourne Bus Depot. It's us lot, at the start of our holiday. Me. Robbie. Dylan. George. So excited. So full of life.

Time seems to be standing still. Gemma keeps on sobbing.

I shut the phone and cram it back in my pocket. I look up at the sky, away from the glare of the moon and out towards the stars and the blackness. My mind is spooling into the future. I start to imagine the pain and disappointment on my mum and dad's faces when I see them. I think about how it's going to be, back on the streets of Letchford. The finger-pointing. The whispering. The strangers knowing who I am and what I've done.

In the space of a few seconds, my whole universe has changed. Nothing's going to be the way I hoped now. This is like a cloud over everything. And it's always going to be there. It seems amazingly, unbelievably unfair.

Tears are welling up in my eyes, but before they can break out I'm feeling disgusted. Ashamed of myself. What sort of bloke am I? Wallowing in self-pity. Whingeing about things not being fair. How fair is all of this for George? My future might not be what I wanted it to be. But George hasn't got a future.

I roll my head from side to side, trying to clear the clutter out of my brain, leave some space for logical thought. It's no good. George is the logical thinker. And he's not around.

"What are we going to do?" I ask.

I don't mean it as a question. But Nikita answers me anyway.

"Look. This is Bellevue Point, right?"

I nod.

"Well I read something in the paper a few months ago. A lad was messing around in a car on the top of these cliffs and he went over the edge. But he survived. He only had a few cuts and bruises. They said it was a one-in-a-million thing. What if it wasn't? What if it's happened again?"

We all look at one another. Maybe George has still got a chance.

"But even if he's alive, we can't get to him," Dylan says, exasperated. "I mean what are we going to do? Abseil?"

"No," Robbie says. "No. We don't need to do that. The steps on the cliff face got swept into the sea years ago, but there's still a way to get down."

Everyone's attention, even Gemma's, fixes on Robbie.

"We'd have to go back towards Whitbourne. There's a path that leads down to a place called Seaward Cove. It's an old smugglers' bay. Hardly anyone ever goes there because it's so difficult to get to, and because the sea comes all the way up to the bottom of the cliffs. When the tide's out though, you can double back along to Bellevue Point. Right underneath where we're sitting."

"But the tide's coming in," Dylan moans.

Gemma's right back with us now.

"We've got to call the Coastguard," she says. "Or the Lifeboats or something. Just dial nine nine nine, get someone to help…"

I'm not listening. I'm on my feet. The burning sensation is leaving me now, being replaced by a coldness. It's like my veins are filling with ice. My body is preparing itself for one massive effort.

"Come on," I say. "The Coastguard will take too long. It's up to us. We've still got time."

fifteen

We're sprinting as we head along the clifftops in the direction of Whitbourne. Robbie's up front, because he knows where we're going, and I'm on his shoulder. Dylan and Nikita aren't far behind. Steph and Gemma are right on their tail. Whatever happens, we're in this together.

We go even faster as the cliff edge sinks into a natural dip. We're flat-out. It's like being on a runaway train. One wrong step now and we'd go tumbling down through the town and out the other side. As we get to the bottom of the dip, Robbie points.

Just past a patch of mangy shrubs and tall grass, is a signpost. It's weathered and warped with an outline of an outstretched finger. The words on the sign have nearly been blasted out of existence by the salty wind but, as we pull level, they're easy enough to decipher. *Seaward Cove.*

I sag forwards with my hands on my knees and blood hammering in my ears. I'm fighting for breath, but I'm still thinking, plotting the next move.

The edge of the cliff is different here. It's not a sheer drop like other parts of the coast. It's more a ragged slope. If I'd ever listened properly in Geography, I could explain how it was formed. An ancient river running to the sea. The track of a glacier. Something like that.

The beach is about sixty metres down. It's half the height of Bellevue Point, but it's still a major trek. A path zigzags right, then left, then right again, disappearing into the darkness. Long slanting steps are cut into the slope, held in place by rough-cut blocks of wood like railway sleepers.

Straightening up, I look around. Determination is written on everyone's faces.

"Ready?" I ask.

They all nod.

I take a breath and start to lead the way downhill.

Although the steps are man-made, nature has been doing its best to reclaim the landscape. As we come round the first corner and cut back in the other direction, the path is already getting dodgy and dangerous. Some of the railway sleepers have fallen away and the ground is uneven and worn. Overgrown weeds and brambles are curving overhead, forming a tunnel. The air is filled with the scent of night-flowering plants and moths are whirring about.

I've been counting the steps, but by the time we're halfway down, I've given up. My mind is wandering. I'm clinging to the hope that George is still alive, but guilt is gnawing at me. How could we have let him down so badly? Big George. Mother Hen. The one who always looked after everyone. Where were we when he needed us? What have we done to him? If the worst comes to the worst, what can we possibly say to his mum and dad?

We're getting near to the end of the climb now. The path is still swinging from side to side, but there's no definition to the steps at all. We're shuffling and sliding, stumbling through the dark, holding on to one another, trying to keep up a good pace. The closer we get to the bottom, the louder the sound of the sea, rushing inland. We cut down to the right one more time and then there's a sharp fork to the left.

The final ten steps to the beach are almost vertical. It's like descending a ladder. I jump the last three rungs and land with a thud. Robbie and Steph are right behind me. Dylan starts to help Nikita and Gemma down.

Seaward Cove is weird. It's not like the coast around the pier and it's not like the bottom of Bellevue Point either. Instead of pebbles or smooth chalk, it's filled with white boulders, stuff that must have fallen from the cliffs over the centuries. All sorts of things have been washed ashore. Bits of smashed boats, broken machinery, ropes, what looks like a whole ship's cargo of hundreds of yellow planks scattered everywhere. The moon is lighting up some parts of the beach and leaving others in shadow. It's like a giant stage set.

Just to the left, there's a pile of mangled metal. It's the remnants of a heavy spiked fence. I suppose it was up at the top of the slope at one stage. I grab hold of one of the rusty poles and wrench it away from the rest. It's about three foot long, solid iron, flat at one end. I swish it around. Something about the weight of it in my hand feels reassuring. I don't know why.

Dylan, Nikita and Gemma are down now, so we press on. There's no discussion. We know what we need to do.

175

It took us about ten minutes to get from Bellevue Point to the top of Seaward Cove. But that was across flat grass. Down here we're weaving through lumps of chalk and heaps of debris, diving across rock pools, trying not to slip on the glistening seaweed. We're cutting through patches of blackness and patches of light. Everyone's totally in the zone, silent and grim, lost in their own little world.

The tide is coming in fast, racing across the beach, whooshing between the boulders. Up ahead, waves are starting to nudge a section of cliff wall sticking out further than the rest. In a night of horrible thoughts, another one has occurred to me. What if the sea gets to George before we do? What if he's survived the fall, but ends up drowning? I keep driving on, faster and faster.

The further away from Seaward Cove we get, the higher the cliffs are towering above us. There's no turning back. I'm way beyond cold. I'm numb. Utterly numb. If you took a sword and ran it through me, I wouldn't feel a thing. The cuts on my hands and knees, the lumps on my head, they're all forgotten about.

We're going as fast as it's possible to go across this ground. But however quickly we go, the sea is quicker. A minute ago it was splashing our feet. Now it's swirling around our ankles. We're not running any more, we're wading. My jeans are saturated. They're heavy, clinging to my legs. There's still no sign of the car, but nobody's panicking. Panicking is no use.

We come round another chalky outcrop and finally the car comes into view. It's fifty metres away, already surrounded by water. It's up to the tops of the wheels and waves are starting to crash across the mangled bonnet and in through the shattered windscreen, carrying on to buffet the base of Bellevue Point.

My body is filled with the burning sensation again. The coldness, the numbness has got me this far. But now reality kicks in. This is life or death.

With a final burst, we splash across to the BMW. The windows are gone and the side panels are gouged and scuffed, but all in all it's in amazingly good condition. It's hard to see, but there only seems to be a few inches of water swilling around in the footwells. The speed the tide is coming in though, another five minutes and the whole interior will be two foot under. And if the interior is underwater, the boot will turn into a death trap.

As a big wave hits the front of the car, I head for the back. Robbie and the others are already there, standing with their eyes fixed on the boot. The lid is dented and scratched and covered in fragments of chalk, but it's in one piece. It's taken the impact of the fall without crumpling. It might have saved George's life.

My heart is pounding like a pneumatic drill. I reach out my hand and try to release the boot lock. I pull the lever but nothing happens. I try again. It's no good. The lid is jammed. I step back, blinking, trying to think what to do next.

Dylan barges me aside and starts jabbing away at the lock, pulling and yanking. He gives up and Robbie has a go.

The water is reaching the middle of my thighs

now, creeping up the side panels of the BMW. More and more is sloshing inside the car. Time is running out. I look at Bellevue Point behind us, rearing up into the night. Then I look down and see what's in my right hand. A three foot, solid iron bar.

"Out of the way," I say.

Robbie's still tugging at the lock, but he's getting nowhere.

"Out of the way," I say again, louder this time.

Robbie doesn't move so I grab his shoulder and push him over to one side. He's surprised and confused but he doesn't resist.

Spinning the iron bar round, I wedge the flat end under the lip of the boot lid and push down as hard as I can. There's a creaking sound, but the metal of the car isn't budging. I try to anchor my feet, get more leverage. It's not easy. My trainers are skidding on the slimy chalk. The iron bar slips out of its groove and I nearly plunge into the churning sea. Getting steady, I try again. This time I work the bar in further, the end disappearing in the narrow gap between the boot lid and the bumper. I push down for a couple of seconds, release the pressure, press for another couple of seconds.

"It's no good," Dylan howls. "It's not going to give."

The water is still rising. A couple more centimetres and it's going to be up to the level of the boot. I lock my hands together and force down on the bar with all the strength I've got left. There's a muffled clunk and the lid pops open a fraction. We're in.

The pounding in my chest has gone. My heart feels like it's stopped. I'm holding my breath, but my senses are on full alert. They're registering every last random detail. Every sight, sound, smell, taste, and texture. This is either going to be the best moment of my life or the worst. It all depends on what I see in the next couple of seconds. Whatever it is, it's going to be with me forever. George could be alive. He could be dead. He could be fine. He could be mangled out of all recognition.

But he's none of those things. Because, as I swing the dented metal lid upwards, he's not there.

I stumble backwards, dropping the iron bar, turning to look at everyone. Dirty, freezing water is rushing in to fill up the boot, but no-one needs to go and check. We've all seen. It's empty.

Steph stretches out her arms. I stagger towards her and we stand swaying with the force of the waves as they drag at our legs, backwards and forwards. My jeans feel like lead weights. Dylan and Robbie are looking at one another, eyes blank. Nikita's staring out to sea. Gemma's got a hand clamped across her mouth.

My brain is motoring at a million miles an hour, trying to get a grip of what's happening. My senses aren't on full alert any more. They're completely scattered. I look at my watch. It's stopped. The water is up to my groin now, and as I glance behind me I start to realise something new. We're trapped. There's no way we can make it back to Seaward Cove and the only way up the cliffs here is the chalk stairway we saw from the top. And that disappears twenty feet above where we're standing. But before there's time for this to sink in, I feel something vibrating against my leg.

I loosen my hold on Steph, reach into my pocket

and get my phone out. It's ringing. I don't bother to check the caller ID. I just slide it open and press it to my ear.

"Alright?" someone says.

My mouth sags open.

"Alright?" the person on the line says again. The voice is sleepy, thick with drink. "Chris? That you?"

My lips start to move, but no sound comes out.

"Who is it?" Robbie asks, face contorting. "Chris? Who is it?"

"It's George," I say.

Everyone looks stunned. Absolutely stunned.

I push the mobile tighter to my ear. I can hardly hear anything over the sound of the waves, but I've got the power of speech back.

"George, where are you? What have you been doing?"

"I don't actually know," George says. "I'm in some little backstreet, trying to find my way to the town centre. I woke up in someone's front garden. I fell over a wall, knocked myself out. There was a concrete eagle lying on the pavement. I must have tripped over it."

I roll my eyes. It's all starting to add up. George never even made it into the car. I feel disgusted with myself, ashamed again. We were all so busy trying to save our own arses that no-one noticed.

"But you're okay, are you?" I ask. "You're really okay?"

"Yeah," George says, surprised I seem so concerned. "Bit of a sore head, but other than that, I'm sound. But anyway, I've been crapping myself. Kirkie's gang were after us weren't they? Or did I imagine that?"

I laugh.

"No George, you didn't imagine it."

I look up. Everyone's mouthing questions at me. I just give them the thumbs-up.

"So where have you got to?" George asks. "Are you all alright? Is Gemma alright?"

I don't know where to start.

"George," I say. "We're all fine. Well, sort of. But if I told you where we were, you'd think I was taking the piss."

"Try me."

I draw a breath.

"We're standing up to our waists in the sea, at the bottom of Bellevue Point, next to a trashed BMW we've pushed off the cliffs."

George has gone quiet.

"Stop messing," he says eventually.

"I'm not messing George. We thought we'd killed you. We thought you were in the boot."

"Shit," George says.

I'm struggling for words again.

"George. George, we thought you were dead, man. But you're not. I can't believe it. When I see you I'm going to give you a kiss. A big sloppy one, right on the lips."

"Eurgh," George says. "Make sure you brush your teeth first."

"Look mate," I say. "Seriously. We're in some proper bother here. We're stranded. We're going to have to call the Coastguard, get the helicopter out. Basically, we've had it. Our mums and dads are going to find out. We're going to have some mega-explaining to do."

"Shit," George says again. "Is there anything I can do to help? Anyone I can call?"

"No George. We've got it covered. The thing is, we can keep you out of this. If you lie low, get the bus to Letchford and go home this evening, no-one needs to know you were involved. We'll make sure your stuff gets back."

George is straight in there. No hesitation.

"Don't be stupid. All for one, one for all. I've just passed the police station. I'll head back and let them know what's occurring in case you can't reach the Coastguard. I'll catch up with you some time later today."

"Yeah, man," I say. "And then we'll never see each other again. Some hardcore bollockings will be going down. We'll all be grounded for the next five years."

George laughs.

"Probably."

"Anyway. Got to go now. We need to get ourselves rescued. See you soon."

"Right," George says. "See you mate. Give my love to Gemma. Keep everyone safe."

"Will do," I say.

I slide the phone shut. I go to put it back in my pocket, but I can't. My pockets are underwater.

We're starting to get knocked about by bigger and bigger waves now, splashed by the spray. The situation is looking pretty ropey, but you'd never know it. We're all grinning from ear to ear. Robbie and Dylan are high-fiving. Nikita and Gemma are hugging one another. Nobody cares that their clothes and shoes are ruined. Nobody cares that we're in for some serious aggro when we get home. It could be a whole lot worse. I'm getting a sense of relief that's so strong it feels like I'm going to explode.

The thing is though, I need to get a grip on myself. The water around us is rising higher and higher. It's going to be up to our necks before too long. Unless we want to drown, we're going to have to swim for the broken stairway. It's the only place we can be safe. I don't need to tell anyone. We've all worked it out for ourselves.

Holding my phone above my head, I lead the way, sculling across to the cliff face. I drag myself onto the crumbling steps, then start hauling everyone else out of the water. Gemma, Nikita, Steph, Dylan and Robbie. When they're all safely behind me, scrambling upwards, I try to take in the entire scene. Everything that's going on. It's beautiful. The moon's reflection on the rippling sea. The pure whiteness of the cliffs. The sparkling stars. I'm actually feeling fantastic. It's the way I felt getting off the coach at Whitbourne Bus Depot. That was thirty-six hours ago. It seems like a lifetime.

Steph is standing one step above me. I pull her close and kiss her. For some reason I'm getting the urge to do somersaults and backflips, dive off the stairway into the sea, but it's not an option. It would wreck my mobile, and I've got an important call to make. We're out of danger for now, but the water level is still on the way up and shows no signs of slowing down.

I slide the phone open and key in the emergency number. I'm ready to hit the connect button, but I'm holding back.

I look up at Steph.

"The minute I send this, a lot of stuff is going to kick off," I say.

Steph nods.

"Not all of it's going to be good is it?"

I shake my head.

For a second Steph looks downcast. Then she squeezes my arm.

"When all this is over, we'll meet up, yeah? You could come down to London or I could come up to Letchford."

"I'd like that," I say. "I'd really like that."

Steph breaks into a smile.

"Right. Consider it sorted," she says. "And you know what? I've got a feeling we're going to be okay."

I grin.

"Yeah. I think you could be right."

I check the digits on the little screen of my mobile. *999*. Glowing in the gloom. With a dab of my thumb, I send the call on its way.

The phone rings once, twice, three times. On the fourth ring there's a click and a woman comes on the line.

"Emergency operator." The voice is calm, businesslike. "Which Service do you require?"

I lick my lips. They taste of salt. I swallow hard.

"Coastguard, please," I say.